DEATH UNDER WRATHFUL SKIES

BLYTHE BAKER

~

A vicious killer haunts the streets of London and has selected a member of Victoria Sedgewick's household as his next victim. Still reeling from recent revelations surrounding her late husband's murder, can Victoria identify this new killer before he claims another life?

The inquiry agent hired by her in-laws still delves into the Sedgewick family secrets, but when violence strikes close to home, Victoria must take matters into her own hands.

~

1

"I am afraid, madam, that there is little choice."

The mess of paper spread out before me, filled with blots of ink and scribbles from scratched out notes, had certainly never done anything to anger me. It was not alive, after all. How could something so simple cause me such great frustration?

It was not the paper itself, of course, but the words upon it. List after list of items, lists that had been altered and added to over and over for the past three hours. Lists that had left me feeling betrayed and vulnerable, something I was none too pleased about.

Perhaps I put undue pressure on the pen in my hand as I squeezed it, staring down at the most recent additions and subtractions from the list. "Why?" I asked. "Of everything that must go, why must those?"

"Because after you returned from your rest at the

seaside, you instructed me to look out for unnecessary expenses, madam. And these are exactly that," said the woman standing beside my desk, examining her own list that was stretched out beside mine.

I knew she had not brought up my short holiday by the sea to make me feel guilty about the expense of it. Still, I admitted to myself that I had taken the trip at a time when I could ill afford to do so. It was as well that I was back in London now.

I looked up at her, and found the same frustration mirrored in her stern face. A face I had looked into many, many times over the years, a face I knew almost as well as my own.

Mrs. Bell, while not the warmest housekeeper, was certainly the most efficient I had ever had.

"Am I to forsake everything that I hold dear?" I grumbled.

"Surely that is slightly dramatic," Mrs. Bell said.

I watched with great sadness as her pen hovered over the words *Pear's soap* before scratching it out. It was as if the nib was scrawling itself over my soul.

I sank back against the back of my chair, a heavy sigh escaping me. "Mrs. Bell, how is changing the soap we use going to save the household money? In the grand scheme of things, it is only going to be a few pence."

"Every bit will help," Mrs. Bell said, writing another brand of soap down beside the newly scratched out name – *Schwartz Soap* – and moving down to the next item on the list.

I glowered over at the letter that lay open across the desktop just a short distance away, still within arm's reach, hoping that the fire in my gaze alone would set it alight. My eyes passed over the words once again, still in disbelief over their content.

My Dear Victoria,

As promised, enclosed is the modified allowance that was agreed upon. I have taken the liberty of deducting a portion to reimburse myself for the funeral expenses. In future, your allowance will return to the following amount.

The amount stated in the letter was a great deal less than what Erasmus, Duncan's father and my father-in-law, had promised originally. What he had sent me was barely enough to survive on, and he was surely well aware of what he had done.

"Mrs. Bell, I do not mean to be a bother, but are you certain about this?"

The voice came from my house cook, Corbyn. The patient, cheery man never failed to put a smile on my face or a warm meal on my table that tasted as good, if not better, than something produced by London's most distinguished chefs.

Corbyn had come up from the kitchen and now stood in the doorway. His arms, visible as the sleeves of his coat had been rolled up in frustration, showed firm muscles from years of kneading dough and carrying wood for the fires. A mop of curling ginger hair crowned his head, and his steady, typically patient eyes were fixed on Mrs. Bell. The list to which he referred was clutched in his hand.

Mrs. Bell huffed as she looked up at him. "On the mistress's orders, I have spent a great many hours going through each and every expense that goes out of this house. This was the kindest I could possibly be, while still maintaining standards."

"But to cut so much..." Corbyn said, shaking his head as he stared down at his list. "Are you certain we can make do with so little?"

"If you are referring to the lesser amounts of imported spices, chocolates, and sugar, then yes, I am certain we can do without," Mrs. Bell said, her eyes flashing. "I am quite sure that the mistress can survive without an elaborate array of sweets. She needs to maintain her health, especially with the little master now beginning to eat more."

I looked behind me at the rather disgruntled infant.

Daniel was nearing six months old now, and was comfortably sitting up on his own. It was hard to believe that he had grown as fast as he had, and was doing exactly as Mrs. Bell had said; eating more solid foods.

Eliza, his nanny, sat before him with a frown on her young face, and a quivering spoon in front of Daniel.

"I'm doing my best, madam..." Eliza said, looking at me with a dismayed expression on her face. "But he just does not seem at all interested in it."

I'm not certain I would be all that interested in mashed peas either...

I turned my gaze up to Mrs. Bell again. "Are you certain all of these cuts must be made?"

"It was your decision that economies must be made, due to limited funds," Mrs. Bell reminded me, tapping the paper with the back of her pen.

I drummed my fingers on the desk, not having the stomach to look at all of the items my housekeeper had suggested we remove from our household necessities. "But now we have one less staff member," I said. "Surely that saves us a great deal in the long-run?"

The footman, Adam, had not been mentioned very often in the weeks that had passed since his death. No one seemed to have the courage to mention his name around me.

Not that I minded, of course. The young man had clearly been dangerously insane and, now that he was gone, I preferred to put all thought of him out of my mind.

Mrs. Bell sighed, pushing her reading spectacles up the bridge of her straight nose. "It does save a little money, his being gone, but not enough."

Though she did not complete the thought, I knew what she was thinking. That the absence of my late husband, Duncan, would prove to be the greatest savings of all for the household. As a hopeless gambler and incurable opium addict, Duncan had frittered away all the inheritance left to me by my parents and much of the allowance supplied by his own father. He would soon have brought us into dire poverty had not his tragic, but convenient, death at the hands of a deranged footman brought his reckless spending to an end.

Yet even the removal of Duncan and Adam, it seemed, was not enough to spare us all an uncertain future.

A soft knock echoed in the room, and my heart skipped. For a moment, I had lost myself and forgotten where I was.

"Come in, yes," I said, turning in my chair to look over at the door.

The aged, wooden door swung inward, and a dark-suited man in his later years stepped in. One might not have known he was older, as he was in perfect condition and more agile than most, but his years were given away by his greying hair.

The butler stood with a straight back, hands clasped tightly behind himself, and bowed deeply to me. "Madam, I know you asked not to be disturbed, but something has occurred that I knew you would wish to be made aware of."

"Oh?" I asked. "To be quite honest, Warrington, I

welcome a bit of interruption. We have not gotten far, and I fear we might be here all evening."

"I certainly hope not," he said. "But here...you should see it with your own eyes."

He walked across the room to me, and laid a newspaper down in front of me.

"I already read this, at breakfast," I said, my brow furrowing.

Warrington shook his head. "This is the evening post. If madam would flip to page three..."

I did as he asked, and felt the eyes of all the others in the room on me. Corbyn had stepped closer to see what it was we were looking at, and Eliza had left Daniel to play with his peas as opposed to eating them.

My eyes swept across the page, and it was only a moment before I realized what it was that had brought Warrington into the study.

An advertisement, perhaps no larger than a calling card, was situated in the bottom right corner of the page.

Persons in need of private inquiry into distressing or inexplicable events should consult V.M. Ward, for discreet and affordable assistance.

I smiled. "I am amazed they printed it. But I suppose, for a fee, one can get anything into the paper."

"Ward is an interesting choice of name, if I may say so," Warrington said.

I nodded. "Yes, well, I could hardly use Duncan's family name, nor my maiden name. It would attract far too much attention, and would likely embarrass my in-laws. As for the initials, my being a lady might turn some away, at first, without giving me the opportunity to prove my capabilities."

"Too true, madam," Warrington said. "This way, they might at least give you a chance."

"That is my hope," I agreed. "Of course, extensive experience is not something I possess yet..."

Briefly, an image flashed through my head, a memory of my late husband's body lying lifeless on the floor.

"Naturally, I have known little of death or violence..." I continued.

Another image, this time of myself holding a murderous footman at bay with a broomstick.

"...However, I am sure I shall prove equal to any tasks set before me. I intend to gather enough cases to, not only cover the difference in what my father-in-law will not pay, but also to create the reputation I need in order to take on higher paying cases in the future."

"It could be lucrative," Corbyn said with a nod.

I gazed down at the ad once again, smiling at the text.

Something out of the corner of my eye drew my attention, then. Another article up at the top of the page, rather long in length, was accompanied by a photograph of a man.

Murder Spree? Or Mere Coincidence? was the title of the article.

"Oh, good heavens..." Mrs. Bell said, glimpsing the article. "Another murder?"

2

"Londinium is a large city, you know," Corbyn said, squinting down at the newspaper sprawled out across the desktop. "Murder should not be much of a surprise."

Our lists lay forgotten beneath the post, our attention entirely focused on the article before us.

I glanced up at Mrs. Bell, whose brow had formed a hard line across her forehead. "What do you mean by another murder?" I asked. "Are you referring to Adam? Or Duncan?"

"No," Mrs. Bell said. "This is someone we do not know at all, it seems."

I noticed her eyes zipping across the page, and I quickly turned my own gaze to the article as well.

Hyde Park, London.

It is just after daylight, the sunlight just beginning to

peek through the trees. The water in the pond is sparkling, and the gentle call of the resident ducks can be heard as they swim together, leaving trails behind them. It is a lovely morning.

Robert Finch (whose name has been changed to protect his identity, as a witness) wanders the park, just as he does every morning around this time. He finds his favorite bench beside the pond where he sits to read his book. This morning may be one of the finest he has seen in weeks.

But something is not right. As Mr. Finch continues to read his book, there is a bone-rattling chill in the air. Something is disrupting his peaceful sanctuary, but he cannot put his finger on precisely what it might be.

"I simply could not relax," he tells writer Jonathon Black in an interview this afternoon. "Something felt wrong, and no matter what I did, I couldn't get comfortable."

When asked what prompted him to rise and search for the source of his unease, he answers, "There were vultures circling overhead a little distance away. I don't typically see them unless they are on the ground, already picking a smaller creature clean...perhaps a squirrel or a rabbit. But they were high over the trees, near a clearing...and something about seeing them sent chills down my spine."

He goes on to say that he arose from his bench and made his way over to where the vultures were circling. "I thought if it was a large enough animal, the authorities might need to be alerted so they could dispose of it if need be..."

The look that passes over Mr. Finch's face is one of terror.

"It was a body, indeed. Not the corpse of an animal...but that of a man."

Mr. Finch tells us that at first, he thought the man might have been sleeping. His body was sprawled out across the grass, after all. "It was almost as if he was looking up at the sky," *Mr. Finch explains.* "It wasn't until I drew nearer that I saw the blood –"

"Madam, if I may," Warrington interrupted my reading. "Are you certain that you wish to read this?"

"Mr. Warrington is right, madam..." Mrs. Bell said. Her face had paled significantly, as she began collecting all of our lists from the desk. "There is no need to distress yourself with such terrible things."

I raised an eyebrow, faintly amused. "Yet all the rest of you have, I see."

Warrington said, "But so soon after the master's death, such details might be too worrying for you."

"Must I remind you that I just put out an advertisement in the very same paper to help others resolve troubling or dangerous situations?" I asked. "I am hardly a delicate flower, unable to bear descriptions of violence. Anyway, now that I am to be a private inquiry agent it would not do me any good to turn my face away from such happenings, would it?"

Warrington inclined his head. "My apologies, madam. You must read whatever you wish, of course."

"Thank you," I said. "I appreciate that you all wish to protect me from unpleasant news, but really my emotions are not as fragile as you think. And how am I to deal with violent situations for potential clients if I am unwilling to read about them in the paper?"

Mrs. Bell, clearly still displeased at the idea, huffed softly as she turned away to collect the rest of our spare papers from the table in front of the sofa.

I shook the newspaper out once again, and continued to read where I had left off.

Mr. Finch explains that the body was found with a gaping hole in the chest, where the heart should have resided. Though blood stained the front of the man's cloth-ing, very little was beneath him. "I imagine he was moved after he was killed," Mr. Finch says. "It was horrifying to see. The body had something unusual fixed to it, as well, a small, thin feather of some sort tucked into the pocket of his jacket."

"A feather?" I murmured. "That's rather peculiar, isn't it?"

"It is indeed," Mrs. Bell said from across the room, evidently unable to resist gossip, even when she disapproved of the subject matter. She was tidying up sofa pillows, and a thin, gauzy tablecloth sat neatly folded atop the side table, perhaps the place where I had spilled my tea the afternoon before. She went on, "It is especially odd, since that seems to be a similarity to two other deaths that have occurred over the past few weeks."

"Truly? Why haven't I heard of such bizarre murders?" I asked, staring at the face of the man portrayed in the photograph. I supposed he must be the witness, Robert Finch, or whatever his real name might be.

"With all of the busyness in the aftermath of Adam's death, as well as the master's, I'm not entirely surprised that you missed hearing of it," Warrington said. "The first death occurred sometime in August and garnered little attention, apart from the fact that it was gruesome. The second death seemed to imitate the first, as the body was found in the same way with the hole in the chest."

"And with the feather," Mrs. Bell said, shaking her head as she pulled a feather duster from some hidden cupboard on the other side of the room and began to sweep it over the bookshelves tucked away in the back corner. "That is three deaths now that have had the same feather on each of the corpses..."

I marveled at the way my butler and housekeeper always seemed to be unending sources of information whenever anything grisly or shocking occurred in the city. There truly was no one so useful as a well-informed servant.

I looked back at the article.

The man who was found dead has been identified as a

Mr. Arnold Locke, a local accountant, well known to members of White's Gentlemen's club, as well as the Athenaeum. A bachelor, he is survived by his parents, Mr. Edward and Mrs. Elizabeth Locke, who also live in London.

The rest of the article denoted some of Mr. Locke's accomplishments, but they mattered little to me in that moment. "How tragic," I said. "To be killed in such a manner..."

"Indeed," Warrington said.

"Three murders..." Mrs. Bell said, shaking her head as she dusted the same spot on the shelf for the third time. "I have heard whispers of these killings all over the city. No one can seem to speak of anything else. It is enough to make one feel unsafe on the streets."

"I shouldn't worry too greatly if I were you, Mrs. Bell," Warrington said with only a hint of mischief. "The murderer seems to be targeting men."

"Yes, of course," Mrs. Bell said, glaring at him. "But how can anyone be certain it will continue that way?"

"You expect there to be more murders?" I asked.

"There certainly seems to be a pattern through all of this, isn't there?" Mrs. Bell asked. "One death could be written off as a lover's quarrel, or perhaps a row between friends. A second, even, could be explained away by some madman being inspired by the newspapers to imitate the first killing. However, a third murder forces one to consider how long this is likely to contin-ue." She shook her head. "There will be rumors flying around, and it will be all the authorities can do to prevent panic."

"What about the other two murder victims?" I asked. "What were they like?"

"The first was a younger fellow," Corbyn said. He'd been quiet, listening to our conversation. "He was found across the street from Hyde Park, in an alleyway. It was suspected that the brutal stabbings to his chest where the result of a fight or robbery. The young man seemed to have a bit of a rough reputation as it was, and so the killing did not attract a great deal of attention."

"And the second?" I asked.

"A man of a more dignified position, if I recall correctly," Warrington said. "Wasn't he an officer of the navy?"

Corbyn nodded. "Yes. A commander, in fact. Widowed and not incredibly wealthy but well liked, it was said."

My cook, it seemed, was every bit as much of an authority on local murders as my butler and house-keeper. I thought with a smirk that if I was not entirely certain of the loyalty of each of them, I should be worried.

I quickly sobered, however, as I stared down at the image of Mr. Locke. "There does not appear to be anything in common between these three men, yet they all wound up dead in the same way, correct?"

Corbyn nodded again. "The second body was found along the bank of the pond inside Hyde Park, and now this Mr. Locke was left somewhere in the middle of the park."

"What is the significance of the park location, I wonder?" I asked.

"I have no earthly idea, but I certainly do not care for it," Mrs. Bell said. "To have these atrocious murders happening so very close to home…"

"Do you expect someone connected with the murder victims might request your help, madam?" Warrington asked.

I frowned. I had not considered the prospect.

"Perhaps someone will," I said. "This is turning out to be quite the big case, isn't it? It's possible some relative of one of these unfortunate men will wish for a private investigation. The police certainly do not seem to have done anything yet."

"That all may or may not occur," Mrs. Bell interrupted. "But in the meantime, we simply must finalize our lists so that this household does not fall apart."

I glared up at her, but there was no denying she was right.

"Yes, Mrs. Bell…" I said sourly. "We shall return to the lists."

Whatever tasks we busied ourselves with, however, I knew that my mind would remain fixed on the mysterious string of murders.

Three days passed, and London strolled into the month of September. It was a beautiful change, with the arrival of cooler nights, more comfortable days, and the promise of holidays and parties in the near future. It was welcome, and the air seemed to buzz with excitement at the coming festivities.

"Christmas is still not for some months," I said over breakfast on the third morning of September. "I'm not certain it is necessary to make arrangements for it already."

"But surely we must begin early, madam?" Mrs. Bell asked as Mr. Tulson served my breakfast.

"Others in town likely already have their plans laid," Warrington agreed with her. "I imagine that the Smiths as well as the Grants will already have their meals planned so their cooks can begin ordering the ingredients they will need."

I looked around. "It isn't as if my home is grand enough for a ballroom, or even a sizable drawing room, for that matter. How can I be expected to entertain guests in such a small setting?"

Warrington said, "You could, of course, choose not to entertain. No one would be surprised, so soon after..."

"So soon after my husband's passing, yes," I finished for him. I glanced down at my dress, which was a deep navy blue. I was not quite in black any longer, but it was still far too soon for any lighter shades. It was true that no one would expect much of me in the way of entertainment this year...

"But no, that will not do," I said aloud. "I will not be seen shutting myself away in a house of mourning forever. I must move on with my life and society must see me do it. By degrees, of course. Nothing too noisy or celebratory."

"Of course, madam. You will throw a small and intimate gathering," Mrs. Bell said. "Everything will be done with the best of taste."

"All right then, it is settled. We shall plan a party for Christmas," I said. "Though I cannot imagine it will be a very merry affair, we shall try and throw off a little of the gloom from this house. I would like my son's first Christmas to be a happy – "

I was interrupted by a sharp rapping sound echoing through the open dining room doors from out in the hall. Someone was at the front door.

"Excuse me, if you will, madam," Warrington said, bowing himself from the room.

"A bit late for the post," I said, returning to my porridge with currants and cinnamon.

My heart skipped suddenly, though, as I realized a very real possibility.

"Mrs. Bell, perhaps it is a letter for V. M. Ward," I said, my eyes widening. "Wouldn't that be splendid if I finally received my first case?"

"Yes, madam. Splendid," Mrs. Bell said with a distinct lack of enthusiasm.

I ignored her attitude. "To be quite honest, I assumed I might have received at least one letter by now. I am beginning to wonder if I shall need to spread my name by word of mouth somehow. Yet, how am I to do that without others knowing it is me?"

"It is a dilemma," my housekeeper agreed. "It will be a challenge, I am sure."

I looked up a moment later as Warrington returned, a letter in his hand. "For you, madam," he said, setting it down beside my pewter plate.

With a sinking feeling, I saw *Mrs. Sedgewick* scrawled across the front of the envelope in swooping letters. Whoever the sender was, they knew it was me, and not some pseudonym I'd chosen for my work as a private inquirer.

I wiped my lips with my napkin before picking it up. The handwriting across the front of the envelope seemed familiar, but I could not place it. I slid open the envelope, unfolded the note, and began to read.

Dear Miss Victoria,

I hope this letter finds you well. I apologize for my lack of communication these past few weeks. I have been caught up in other business that demands my time and energy. I wish to assure you, however, that your matter has not been forgotten, and I am doing what I can to get to the bottom of it all.

"Ah, Mr. Keats," I said.

"The detective?" Mrs. Bell asked, with interest. "I wonder what he wants now?"

Mr. Branwell Keats was a private inquiry agent my father-in-law had hired to investigate the death of Duncan. In fact, Mr. Keats had been the inspiration behind my idea of taking up detective work myself, though he did not know that. He seemed a capable enough man, but it had struck me at the time of the investigation that anything he could do, I was just as capable of, as well.

I decided there was no harm in indulging Mrs. Bell's curiosity.

"The authorities may consider the matter of my husband's death to be resolved, but Mr. Keats has other ideas," I said. "Before Adam's death, he said something to me that implied he might not have been acting entirely alone in the murder. It sounded as if someone else had suggested the idea to him. And if so, he died without divulging the name of that mysterious person. Naturally, I would like to learn that name. Mr. Keats, too, is interested in digging a little further."

Mrs. Bell shuddered. "Someone put Adam up to it? Who could do such a thing?"

I shrugged my shoulders. "As I've said, there is no knowing, at least not yet. And it may all prove to be nothing. Adam's description of events made it unclear whether the mystery person even knew who Duncan was or that Adam was a servant in our home. It could have been entirely random.'"

"But you wish to be sure," Mrs. Bell said.

"Exactly. I cannot put the matter fully from my mind, until I am satisfied," I said. "Mr. Keats, I hope, may be able to learn a little more."

I continued reading the letter.

I have spent a great deal of time going through a number of suspects that I think might be responsible. It seems your husband had quite a long list of places he would frequent, and it has taken time to visit them all and speak with those in charge. Some remembered him, others did not, which of course added another layer of difficulty –

"Come now, man, just tell me if you've learned anything," I muttered, frowning down at the paper.

One thing is certain; whoever wished your husband dead truly does not want to be found. It is as if this person left no trace.

There remains hope, however. Even the most skilled of villains always forgets something. They always make a mistake or leave something behind. Even if it takes a great deal of effort and patience, that one small error can be found and exploited to reveal the truth.

I will find that error, Miss Victoria, and we will bring this person to justice.

In the meantime, I believe I might be on to something, a new trail I have yet to follow. I cannot be sure, but I will send you further reports when I know more.

I hope you and your son are in the best of health.

Sincerely,

Branwell Keats.

I scowled down at the letter.

"What is the matter, madam?" Mrs. Bell asked. "Is the news bad?"

"No," I said. "It is no news at all, because I cannot even be certain that he has learned anything. It is nothing more than cryptic hints and allusions to progress. He thinks he might have a lead, but he cannot be certain. And he will not even tell me what the lead might be."

I tossed the letter aside, annoyed.

Does he think so little of me that he will not bother to

tell me what it is he's found? Or am I just too simple minded
to know the truth about his discoveries?

"I do not know why the man writes at all, if he has
nothing useful to say," I grumbled. "Does he not think
I have a right to take an interest in this matter, a right
to know the full details?"

Mrs. Bell said, "Perhaps he will not tell you
anything else because he truly knows nothing more?
That would seem a logical conclusion."

I furrowed my brow at her, knowing she might very
well be correct, regardless of whether or not I liked it.

"Warrington, please fetch me some paper and a
pen," I said. "I believe Mr. Keats needs to know that I
received his letter and that I am none too pleased with
being left in the dark."

My butler departed the room, leaving me alone
with Mrs. Bell and Mr. Tulson.

"What?" I asked Mrs. Bell, recognizing the disap-
proving expression on her face.

"Forgive me, madam, but is it wise to question the
inquirer like that?" she asked. "He is investigating
further into the late master's death, after all. And you
need not pay for it."

I drummed my fingers on the table.

I still found myself rather annoyed that the letter
had not come from someone else, seeking help on a
case of some sort. Eager to separate myself from my
dreaded in-laws, I wanted nothing more than for my

business to succeed so that I could provide for my little family all on my own. I did not want old Erasmus's help...or lack thereof.

"I suppose I see your point," I admitted. "I do not wish to distract Mr. Keats from his work. Yet I do wish to discover who might have wanted Duncan dead enough that they urged Adam into action."

"It is certainly a troubling question," Mrs. Bell said.

"I imagine it could be someone he crossed in a gambling hall or public house," I mused. "There could be any number of people unknown to me, who had a grudge against him."

It wasn't as if I had not contemplated looking into the matter myself, of course, and I might well do so if Mr. Keats failed to turn up information any time soon. However, something held me back. I had not hesitated to investigate Duncan's death immediately after it took place. But discovering the killer had been a member of my own household had rattled me, even before I learned that Adam might have been acting partially under the influence of someone else.

Yes, I found myself strangely reluctant to touch the matter again, as if I were too close to it. Duncan's death was too personal to leave me unaffected, and so, I had chosen to distance myself from it. At least for the present, I would rely on Mr. Keats to do his own digging and keep me informed from a distance.

Warrington returned a few moments later, and I

happily took the paper and pen from him, pushing aside my half-eaten breakfast.

"What do you intend to write?" Mrs. Bell asked, as Warrington placed a bottle of fresh ink on the table beside me.

"I intend to inform Mr. Keats that I did not appreciate his refusal to give me solid information," I said. "I feel as if I deserve to know more about what he is investigating than what he is letting on thus far."

I position my pen over the paper, and pressed the nib to it until the ink began to run freely.

Mr. Keats,

Thank you for your letter. Both my son and I are in good health, thank you for asking.

I paused for a moment, staring down at the letter.

Now that I was writing it, what was I going to say?

I had every intention just a few moments before of making a firm request for the information I sought. For far too long, I had been in the dark, and I was ready for solid answers in some regard.

However, as I sat there, I realized that I could be as demanding as I wished, but the truth was that it was my in-laws, and not I, who paid the private detective's fees. Mr. Keats, courteous though he may be, was free to ignore everything I said, and there was nothing I could do about it.

So in a moment of decision, I changed my mind.

I wonder if you might be available to meet so that you

and I could further discuss the matter of my late husband's death. I am grateful to be kept informed on the matter of your continued investigation, and I would be very intrigued to hear more about your findings in greater detail.

"You know, madam..." Warrington said. "I do wonder if he neglected to put any further information in his letter to you because it would have been unwise."

"How so?" I asked.

"Quite simply, what if the letter was intercepted?" he asked. "If he named names, or gave you more information about the ins and outs of his investigation, might it put you in harm's way?"

I pursed my lips, staring down at the letter.

"You do not think this was his way of keeping me out of it?" I asked.

"It may or may not be," Warrington said. "But it is equally possible that caution kept him silent."

"Perhaps a meeting would be wise, then," I mused. "He could be more willing to explain himself further when there is no risk of letters being intercepted."

I furrowed my brow, not liking the next thought that intruded into my mind. "Of course, there is another option I have been trying my best not to consider. It is entirely possible that Mr. Keats's lack of cooperation will force me into investigating this matter myself. I've proved myself capable enough before, after all."

Mrs. Bell seemed to sense my reservations, though I didn't speak them aloud. "But surely it would be distressing for you, madam, resurrecting the memories of the late master's death? Resolving the troubles of paying clients is one thing, but would you truly wish to return to such a personal case?"

"I do not see that my wishes enter into it much," I said. "I have been trying to put off the matter, to leave it to Mr. Keats, but it now appears he makes no progress. Or if he does, he is reluctant to share it. Either way, it seems the time may have come for me to take things into my own hands."

Mrs. Bell looked troubled. "This could involve more danger than any you have confronted before."

"I understand your concern," I said. "But the opportunity to gain wider experience is precisely why I wonder if I should attempt this on my own. I have not been hired for any cases of my own yet, so why shouldn't I try? Would it not be a good way for me to increase my credibility?"

"If I may say so, madam, it could be more difficult than you expect," Warrington put in diplomatically. "Surely you have a great deal less to go on? And I am sorry to point out that you do not have the same resources or contacts that Mr. Keats undoubtedly has."

I frowned. "I had not considered that..."

Mr. Keats certainly did have more resources than I. He likely had well established connections he could rely on, as well as people who would be able to do some of the dirty work that he wasn't able to.

These were all advantages I lacked, and it would likely be a long time before I could change that.

"I suppose you are right," I acknowledged. "Still, I believe asking for a meeting is prudent. Mr. Keats is a reasonable man, and there is every chance he will be willing to discuss what he has found, once we see one another face to face."

I spoke with confidence, but it was no match for the nagging doubts I carried inside.

4

———

Nearly a week had passed, and still I had yet to receive any contact from potential clients seeking my assistance. Every morning I checked the paper, wondering if my advertisement was still being printed, and every morning I found it in the same location, down at the bottom of the third page.

Whenever Warrington went to fetch the post, I stared after him, hopefully. Would today bring the first case I needed?

It never did, however.

"I need some fresh air," I informed my servants abruptly at breakfast one morning. "I think I am going to take Daniel and go for a walk down to the park."

"What a splendid idea, madam," Mrs. Bell said. "The weather looks beautiful this morning, and the little master will likely enjoy some time out of the house."

I pushed the beans around on my plate. Since Mrs. Bell had implemented the economies we had discussed, the meals Corbyn had been able to prepare in the kitchen were a great deal less enjoyable than they typically were. Mrs. Bell insisted on more afford-able ingredients, and had also instructed some of the staff to create plans for a garden come spring. In the meantime, my meals were becoming increasingly less interesting. Even my tea had been greatly reduced. I was only able to enjoy it in the afternoon, with only two cups at best.

The past week had been uneventful, and I had done nothing productive aside from going through Mrs. Bell's lists even further to ensure that we had really cut everything possible from the household.

I had even found myself going through my jewelry box, locating brooches and necklaces that I had not worn in several years. Warrington offered to take them down to the jeweler to be appraised. The sale of the items brought in some money, but it wasn't going to be enough to live on for long.

"Eliza?" I asked now, looking over at the nurse who was hovering near Daniel and feeding him mashed carrots.

"Yes, madam?" she asked.

"You will accompany me on my walk this morn-

ing," I said. "We shall prepare as soon as the baby is
finished eating."

"Yes, of course," she said. "I think he is finished
now."

I disliked being so particular about my food, especially since the changes to the menu had been partially
my own idea, but I pushed my plate away from me
regardless. "I am finished as well, and eager to be out
of doors. Please change Daniel and we will be on our
way."

Eliza readied him in a comfortable outfit, along
with a warm jacket, as there was a breeze that morning.
Warrington prepared the baby carriage, and fetched
my parasol.

We set off from the house at half past nine, when
the sun still washed over the streets, and the bite in the
air from the previous night had all but fled.

I adjusted the parasol over my shoulder as Eliza
pushed the baby carriage along. I'd chosen one of the
few riding dresses I still possessed, one made of a deep
green with dark lace adorning the collar and cuffs of
the sleeves. It was suitably somber for a widow, yet still
fashionable. The very last thing I wished to convey to
the public was that our household had fallen upon
hard times, and that it was likely going to be some time
before I could afford such luxurious clothing again.

Eliza strolled along beside me, wearing her simple
dress with matching bonnet, and keeping a watchful

eye on Daniel. Like me, she seemed to be more careful than ever with the infant, since his father had died.

"He's just fine, Eliza," I said, pointing down at the wriggling baby inside the carriage. "He is quite content."

Daniel clasped at the blanket tucked in over the top of him, cooing as he batted his long eyelashes up at me.

"Indeed, he seems to be," Eliza said. "And my, what a lovely morning it is, isn't it, madam?"

I looked around us. Mayfair was one of the finest parts of London, which was why I had always loved my aunt and uncle's home there. I knew it was because of my connection with them that Duncan and I had been able to find a home in the area in the first place.

The townhouses up and down the street all looked similar, quite stately in nature, all made from the same rich red brick, with wrought iron fences separating each lot from the next, as well as fencing in the lower windows sunken down below the sidewalk. Each home had many windows that overlooked the street below, all framed in the same thick slabs of limestone.

It would have been easy to become lost in the maze of streets and homes that were so alike. But having lived there for some years now, finding my way about had become second nature, the streets almost as familiar as those surrounding the home my parents had owned in Knightsbridge where I had been raised.

We were not the only ones out enjoying the weather today, it seemed. Couples strolled up and down the street, men in their high collar jackets and top hats, and ladies in their flowing silk dresses.

"Good morning, Mrs. Reese, Mrs. Cooper," I said as we passed a pair of ladies standing at the foot of the stairs just a few houses down.

The elderly ladies turned to look at me. Mrs. Reese, a woman whose hair remained shockingly black for her years, let out a sound of surprise. "Oh, Mrs. Sedgewick," she said in her high, small voice. "How lovely it is to see you, my dear. I was beginning to think you had become a hermit, with how little we see of you these days."

"Not quite, Mrs. Reese," I said, motioning for Eliza to slow the baby carriage to a stop. "I thought little Daniel and I would take advantage of the lovely day and make our way down to Hyde Park for some exercise."

Mrs. Reese's eyes, a clear shade of blue, widened. "Oh, good heavens, are you certain you wish to go there? Isn't it where that terrible murder occurred so recently?" she asked.

"That was nearly a week ago now," pointed out Mrs. Cooper, a rather boorish woman with respect only for those above her in station. "The fellow's remains have long since been cleared away. You would never know anything had happened there now."

Mrs. Reese shuddered nonetheless, and looked back at me, as if eager to change the subject. "How are you, dear? I hope your spirits are improving a little after...well, everything that has occurred."

"I am well enough, I suppose," I said, allowing a tone of sadness to enter my voice. I did not wish to be seen as cold or uncaring after Duncan's death. These women would not understand how troubled my marriage had been, and it would not do my reputation any good to be seen as heartless. I added, "It has all happened so quickly, it's been rather difficult to accustom myself to it."

"But you are well?" Mrs. Reese asked. "Living in that big house, all alone..."

"Oh, I am hardly alone," I assured her. "I have my staff to manage the house and, of course, there is my Daniel."

Mrs. Reese looked down into the carriage, her bottom lip protruding. "Oh, look at him...how sweet he is. So well behaved, as well."

"He is indeed," I said.

I felt Mrs. Cooper's gaze on me, and when I met her eye, I thought for certain that she might ask a question. The moment passed, however, when she shifted her attention to Mrs. Reese. "Come along, Violet. We wouldn't want to be late for Mrs. Kensington's luncheon." She gave me a brief, flashing look out of the corner of her eye as she mentioned Mrs. Kensington.

"Of course," Mrs. Reese said. "Now, do be careful down at the park, Mrs. Sedgewick. There is no telling what sort of foul things are afoot in this city as of late."

"I certainly will be watchful, Mrs. Reese," I said. "And please give Mrs. Kensington my best, won't you?"

Mrs. Reese nodded as Mrs. Cooper pulled her along back down the street, away from me.

"Good heavens..." I muttered, the smile on my face falling away at once. "Mrs. Cooper could not have made it any more clear what she thinks of me."

It was true. The woman had always made it known that she disapproved of my marrying Duncan, and now there she was, pretending as if she was somehow of higher status than I. Almost as if she guessed at my financial difficulties.

My nerves sang as we pushed the carriage along the sidewalk past more people who were carrying on about their days.

It was infuriating, having to live this way. I was well aware that money was not everything, but when my family's wealth was robbed from me by my spendthrift husband...

I bit down on my tongue to keep myself from going any further down that route. I was angry, yes, but I did not need to show it in my expression and allow everyone else to see the sort of predicament I was in.

There was always the option that I could leave Mayfair, I thought, looking up at all of the buildings around me. I imagined there would be simple, yet respectable, housing somewhere in London that might be more affordable for a lady in my changed circumstances. But there was my reputation to consider, and my son's future. A move to cheaper accommodations would affect our social status and make it all too clear that we had come down a rung in the world. There was no telling what sort of opportunities that could cost Daniel as he grew older, to say nothing of the embarrassment it would cause me.

Yet the only hope I could see of avoiding such a thing was if my new business venture became a success. Preferably very soon. That might enable me to keep the house and stay in Mayfair. But what else could I do to attract the attention of potential clients? Short of standing on the street corner with my advertisement in hand, I was truly uncertain how I might attract notice.

We came to a corner, which Eliza and I stopped at to allow a few horses and carriages past. A newspaper boy called out from the opposite corner of the street near a florist's, and on the eastern side of the street, I watched as people sat outside a tea house and sipped from delicate china cups and enjoyed small plates of sandwiches and baked goods.

I bristled, longing in that moment to be able to go and sit down without a care, and be able to have my fill of sweets and tea.

"I wonder if my father-in-law meant to put me in such dire straits," I muttered to Eliza. "If he meant for me to feel as if we are drowning. I realize that I am hardly paying you what you are owed, along with the rest of my staff – "

"It's all right, madam," Eliza said nervously, as she pushed the baby carriage along. "We have all agreed to stay with you, even if we must endure some time without pay – "

I came to an abrupt halt. "And what if I cannot pay you anything? Will you stay with me indefinitely, out of your loyalty alone?"

Eliza's gaze flickered to the side, and she hesitated for just a moment.

"As I thought," I said, starting forward once more as we continued on up the street toward the park. "And I do not blame you in the least. It cannot continue this way. Old Mr. Sedgewick means me to beg him for more money, so that I will remain aware of my dependence upon him. But I will not allow him and Hudson to manipulate me. I will find a solution of my own. My staff deserve to be paid, and I intend to ensure they are...somehow."

"Thank you, madam," Eliza said uncertainly. "You are too kind."

We came to another intersection, taking a left turn, and as we continued to walk, I did my best to think of ways in which to do more with the advertisement I'd already made. "Perhaps putting it in shop windows?" I asked aloud. "Or sending Mr. Tulson to hand out flyers in the streets in order to garner more attention?"

"All of those sound like splendid ideas, madam," Eliza said with an adamant nod of her head.

I gave the nanny a dissatisfied frown. "Eliza, sometimes I wonder if you only agree with me because I am your employer."

The girl's eyes widened. "Oh, no, of course not, madam."

I arched a brow. "Very well. But your timidity knows no bounds, it seems..."

The grandiose homes and shops soon gave way to the beautiful green landscape that was Hyde Park. The stale smoke in the air seemed to thin, and the leaves fluttered in the gentle breeze sweeping through the city. The sounds of horse hooves and their drivers carried across the streets, as well as the general hustle and bustle from the city itself.

"Come along, Eliza," I said. "Keep up, keep up."

We hurried across the street as the carriages drove past. Many ladies were in their finery, enjoying one of the last weeks without the need for cloaks or shawls. Winter may have been some weeks away, but the first hints of it were reflected in the edges of the leaves that had begun to change in a tree or two.

Daniel's eyes peered around as he attempted to sit up in his carriage.

"Yes, I know, dear, it's all very exciting," I said, looking about. "Wait until we are in the park. Then perhaps we will see some ducks, or perhaps a swan or two."

A well-dressed gentleman tipped his hat at me as we passed, and for a moment, I had the odd thought that it might have been Mr. Keats. He had the same dark hair and mustache as the private inquirer, after all.

But when I turned to look over my shoulder, he had already disappeared back amongst the crowd.

No, I'm certain that was not him. Why ever did I imagine it might have been?

There was a rather simple answer to that. I had matters to discuss with Mr. Keats. In a way, this would be a convenient time and place to run into him, and so it was no surprise that my imagination had conjured him up.

As soon as we crossed the streets and stepped foot into the park, the trees seemed to absorb the sounds of the city. Instead of the clacking of wheels on the cobbles, we heard the chirp of birds as they flew from limb to limb, enjoying the morning just as we were.

The further we walked, the more peaceful the world around us became. Long stretches of grass filled the space between the wandering paths, where children played games and chased one another in circles. People strolled along the paths, their heads bent together in quiet conversation. A young couple had spread blankets across the ground and shared a picnic, entirely oblivious to anyone but themselves.

"It's almost as if we are in the countryside, isn't it, madam?" Eliza asked. "It's so quiet this deep into the park."

"Indeed it is," I said. "One of the best parts of this city, if you ask me."

Soon after, I decided to take Daniel out of his carriage so that he could look around at all of the people and the dogs playing. He seemed most interested in a flock of geese that were waddling across the path, their back ends wiggling as they walked.

"He is quite intrigued by those birds, isn't he?" Eliza asked.

"He certainly seems to be," I said with a chuckle. "He always seems to enjoy the birds that visit the feeder outside our – "

My words were lost beneath a sudden scream that echoed all throughout the park.

∾

IT WAS as if I'd been dipped in icy water. I froze, as did Eliza beside me. Even poor Daniel stiffened, his head spinning in the direction the terrible sound had come from.

The world itself seemed to stand still. The couple

on the blanket had shifted to look off into the distance.
People walking up and down the paths alongside us
had stopped, staring around. Children ceased their
games, and some of the younger ones ran to their
mothers.

"What was that?" I asked under my breath, but as
soon as the words passed over my lips, movement
appeared between the distant trees.

A young woman barreled out of a cluster of trees
some distance away from the path. Her face was
horror-struck, her hat slightly askew. She clutched at
her skirts as she ran, nearly stumbling as her shoe
caught against a large root protruding from the
ground.

She did not seem to care. Gasping for air, she
hurried away as fast as her legs would carry her.

It was not a moment later before a young man
around her age hurried out after her, holding his top
hat tightly against himself.

The woman ran to another couple standing alongside the path, and as soon as she reached them, she
burst into tears, and began carrying on hysterically.

"Poor dear, I wonder what she is saying," Eliza said
with a frown.

My eyes narrowed as I watched her, attempting to
discern what it was she was saying to the couple. "She
saw something," I said.

The woman pointed behind her at the trees as the

young man reached her. The other man, who they had run to, a person somewhat older than they, furrowed his brow as he looked between them. The younger man with the top hat pressed against himself nodded.

"He's dead!" wailed the young woman. "Dead, I tell you!"

Murmurs from the crowds around me began to stir, and the unease in the air only increased.

"Someone is...dead?" Eliza asked beside me, breathless.

Fear rooted me to the spot for a moment. *Not again. These sorts of terrible tragedies seem to be following me around...*

And yet...

Wasn't this the sort of opportunity I was looking for? I was here at the scene of a crime, was I not? Perhaps this would be the perfect chance for me to demonstrate the skill I knew I possessed.

"Eliza, please take Daniel," I said, holding the infant out to her.

She took him at once, although he appeared none too pleased to have moved further away from the geese that seemed entirely oblivious to the frightened humans standing around them. "What are you going to do, madam?" she asked.

"I am going to go and discover what has happened," I said. "I believe I might have found the opportunity I have been looking for."

5

Eliza looked fearful. "That woman is claiming someone is dead," she said. "Are you certain you wish to go closer, madam?"

"It will hardly be the first death I have seen," I said. "And I imagine, if I am to indeed take on cases as a private inquirer, it will not be my last."

"But what if – " she protested.

"It's quite all right, Eliza," I said firmly. "I shall not be gone long."

I turned away before the girl could protest further.

I realized a moment later that I was not the only one slowly making my way over to the cluster of trees the young man and woman had fled from. Another person, a man likely in his late forties or early fifties, wearing a crisp blue suit, was already halfway there.

He seemed to have no fear. Perhaps a man of the military?

A few more curious onlookers had moved closer, but no one seemed quite brave enough, apart from the man in blue, to cross into the shadows of the trees.

I hovered near the closest trunk, my curiosity strong enough that it urged me to peer around and into the clearing. I steeled myself, hearing gasps and whispers behind me, as I walked out from behind the tree.

There was indeed a man's body upon the ground, lying entirely still, as if he'd simply fallen asleep there, sprawled out on his back.

He wore a simple black suit, which obscured some of the blood that seeped out of a gaping wound in his chest. The white shirt – at least, I believed it must have been white at one point in time – was so saturated it had turned almost entirely red. All except the collar had been stained.

The wound was just off center, precisely where his heart would be. I found myself grateful that it was difficult beneath the shadows of the trees to make out the details of the wound. The last thing that caught my eye was a white feather, small and thin, tucked into the lapel pocket of his suit coat.

It is just as the newspaper described the last murder...

For a wild moment, I wondered if the police had never come into the park to remove that last body, for this seemed to be almost the exact same scene painted in the paper. But of course, that was impossible. This must be an entirely different victim.

For a moment, I felt slightly ill, but then I reminded myself that I was already uniquely experienced to deal with this sort of thing. And I would have to keep a strong stomach, if I intended to make a living of investigating all sorts of crimes.

This isn't Duncan, and this isn't Adam. I do not know this person. If I am going to take this on as a case, then I must *look at him more closely.*

The man in blue was there, already crouched beside the still body, examining it. He was more trim and fit than I had originally thought. His hands were working hands, and he kept his salt and pepper hair short, like his silver moustache.

As I approached, he turned to look at me.

"Miss, this could be too distressing for a lady such as yourself," he said in a rumbling voice that held authority. "It would be best for you to wait out in the clearing."

I stood straighter, having no intention of being intimidated. "Thank you for your concern, but I am fully capable of managing my...*distress*. I happened to be in the park and heard that young woman scream. I thought it best to lend my help, if needed."

The man in blue looked startled for a moment, and he took a closer look at me.

My unruffled demeanor must have convinced him, because he nodded.

"Very well, though I fear it is too late to lend any help to this poor fellow," he said.

I peered down at the body. "Yes, I dare say he is long past medical assistance. Still, he might receive some measure of justice if whoever perpetrated this crime is caught. I work, you see, as a private inquirer."

It was the first time I had ever spoken the words, but I said them with confidence all the same.

"A private inquirer, hmm?" he asked. "And a woman, no less? Well, I should have guessed something was different about you. You didn't seem to fear a corpse the same way others might."

"Yes, I have seen my fair share of them," I said.

The man stood to his feet and extended his hand. "My name's Holmstead. I'm with Scotland Yard.

"Scotland Yard, you say?" I asked.

I took his hand and shook it, as a man would, wondering if there was significance to the gesture. Perhaps it was his way of signaling that he saw me as a professional, rather than as a lady? If so, I was grateful for the brisk courtesy.

"Well, aren't we fortunate that you happened to be taking a morning stroll through the park?" I asked.

"Indeed..." he said, his eyes falling down again to the man lying on the ground before us. A rather peculiar look came over him, but he cleared his throat and looked about. "Well, I shall have to send for assistance and ask those who discovered the dead man to remain behind for questioning. Miss...what did you say your name was?" he asked.

"Ward," I answered, mechanically. "My name is Miss Ward."

He nodded. "Very well, Miss Ward. In light of your experience, your presence here is convenient. Perhaps you would be good enough to collect the names of witnesses, while I go and call for reinforcements?"

"Yes, of course," I said. "Anything to move things along efficiently."

I followed the man called Holmstead from the clearing, and he gave me nothing but a small nod before making his way over to the young woman who had fled the clearing, who still stood with the other couple, the older woman embracing the younger one.

I did as I had been asked, and made my way around to the various bystanders, those whose curiosity had brought them nearer to observe and learn what they could. I collected all their names and asked them to remain where they were, as the police would be arriving soon and would very likely have questions for anyone who might have seen anything out of the ordinary.

This sort of task was not what I'd expected to be doing as a private inquirer, but it seemed that it was a perfectly good way of getting my name recognized.

More than one person asked for my name, to which I happily replied, "Miss Ward."

Not a lie, but a pseudonym. The city of London, as vast and as populated as it was, was the perfect sort of place to have another name with which to begin my new business. It would ensure that my private life remained quiet, and yet would also keep my father-in-law out of my personal doings. He wouldn't recognize the name Ward, and it would spare him and the rest of my extended relations any embarrassment. I felt safe in assuming none of them would care to have a lady private inquirer in the family, especially one who advertised her services in the newspapers. Yes, if "Mrs. Sedgewick" was to maintain any privacy, I would have to get used to being "Miss Ward" at times.

When I had finished collecting the bystanders' information, I turned it over to Holmstead a short time later, and then I returned to Eliza and the baby.

"Madam, what is happening?" Eliza asked as I reached her and Daniel.

Daniel, who seemed to be quite inconsolable, reached out to me as I approached, fat tears rolling down his cheeks.

"Oh, hush now, little one..." I said, taking him in my arms and bouncing him. I looked up at Eliza. "Well, it seems there is now a fourth murder akin to the others that have happened recently."

Her eyes widened. "You do not mean – "

I nodded, glancing over my shoulder in the direction of the clearing. "It is in the same fashion as the three before it. The wound in the chest, the white dove feather in the pocket...and now, I believe, all four of the deaths have occurred in or around Hyde Park."

"That's terribly bizarre, is it not?" Eliza asked, rubbing her arms nervously as she followed my gaze. "All four in the same location?"

"It is indeed," I said.

"If you don't mind my asking, who was that man you were speaking with?" Eliza asked. "The one you came out of the clearing with?"

"That was Mr. Holmstead," I said. "He is with Scotland Yard."

"Scotland Yard?" she asked. "So the authorities are now involved?"

"They have been involved since the beginning," I said. "But I imagine with four murders, all very similar in nature, they will be taking the time to investigate much further into the matter than they may have before."

It seemed I was correct in that prediction. After a short time of waiting, a group of men in dark blue coats appeared, and made their way directly to the body in the clearing.

"That would be the police," I said, noting their hats.

I saw one of the more senior officers, with buttons of polished silver, speaking with Holmstead.

"What will they ask us?" Eliza asked. We had taken refuge on a bench near the path.

Daniel had fallen asleep in his carriage, which I rocked back and forth to ensure his rest would be as long as possible.

"What we saw, mostly," I said. "Which was not a great deal, apart from the woman running out of the trees, and the young man after her."

"Oh, madam," Eliza said suddenly. "Isn't that Mr. Keats? The detective who used to come to the house after the master died?"

I turned, surprised to see a familiar figure standing with some of the constables, nodding his head.

His top hat, black with a white ribbon wrapped around it, sat atop his dark hair, and his tall, lean frame and broad shoulders gave him away.

"Yes, I believe you are right," I said, shifting uncomfortably in my seat. "That is indeed Mr. Keats."

Now what am I to do? There are two private inquirers here? I certainly hope he doesn't get a chance to speak with Mr. Holmstead...

I wasn't sure why, but I felt strangely possessive of this case I had stumbled upon. This was my opportunity to prove myself and I did not want Mr. Branwell Keats stealing it from me. For that matter, I could not be sure how he would react to the discovery that I was in the process of entering his own field.

Then the thought struck me. If I were to get his attention before Holmstead did, then I would be able to prevent any sort of conversation between the men from ever coming up in the first place.

I did my best to keep my gaze focused on him. If he felt my eyes, then perhaps he –

Well done, Mr. Keats.

His gaze shifted away from the constables, and scanned the crowds that had been asked to stay nearby. It only took him a moment before his grey eyes fell upon me, and widened.

He excused himself from the constables and started over toward us.

"Oh, good heavens, He is coming right toward us," Eliza said.

"Remain calm, Eliza," I said, waving kindly at Mr. Keats. "If we manage to be questioned first, then perhaps we can leave here without Holmstead introducing Mr. Keats and I to one another, both as inquirers. I imagine Mr. Keats might find that information... well, rather interesting."

"Mrs. Sedgwick," Mr. Keats said in his clear, crisp tone, as he tipped his hat.

"Mr. Keats," I greeted him in return. "As I told you when last we met, you may call me Miss Victoria now.

It is not so long ago that I went by that name, before my marriage."

"If you prefer it," he said. "Then may I wish you a good afternoon, Miss Victoria?"

"Is it a good afternoon, when yet another unfortunate man has been killed?" I asked.

He tilted his head. "I suppose it depends on whether one is in his position or ours."

I looked past him at the clearing. "I assume they have called you in to help with this case?" I asked.

"Indeed they have," he said. "It seems that four deaths of the same nature warrant outside assistance. I am happy to earn my fee, of course, yet I cannot help but worry that this might be one of the more difficult cases I have ever taken on."

"Indeed?" I asked. "Why is that?"

He gave me a steady look, a flicker of amusement passing over his face. "Miss Victoria, how is it that you and your servant both happened to be here in the park when a dead body was discovered?" he asked. "If I were not a discerning man, I might have my doubts about you, given the recent history of deaths at your own home..."

I arched an eyebrow. "I hardly think this is an occasion for jesting, Mr. Keats."

"It was not entirely a jest. You must understand, Miss Victoria, that asking such questions is a part of my job. If I do not ask them, then who will?"

I hid my irritation and folded my hands calmly in my lap. "In that case, allow me to answer. As you know very well, I live nearby," I said. "Not more than a quarter of an hour's walk from the edge of Hyde Park. Clearly, I was not the only person who wished to take advantage of the lovely weather we had today." I gestured around at all of the other families and couples that were now being questioned by various members of Scotland Yard.

"Indeed," Mr. Keats said, looking over his shoulder. "Though I know full well a lady of your reputation could not be involved in such a heinous crime, I must say your timing is quite curious."

"The very same thought passed through my own mind," I said. "It seems that I have a knack for being in unfortunate places at unfortunate times."

"Was there anything suspicious that you noticed on arriving at the park?" Mr. Keats asked.

"Not at all," I said. "Eliza and I arrived only a few moments before we heard a terrible scream, and saw that young woman bolt out of the trees in hysterics." I pointed to the woman in question, who was now surrounded by three constables and clearly on the verge of tears once more. "She was closely followed by the young man there in the green."

"I see," Mr. Keats said, pulling a small book from the inner pocket of his coat, and beginning to scrawl notes inside.

"What of the victim?" I asked. "Do the authorities know who he is?"

"Not yet, no," Mr. Keats said, glancing briefly up at me. "I am certain we are all quite eager to know, however."

"I did not see any wedding ring on his hand," I said. "I should think if he has no wife, then it may take a little more time for someone to notice his absence from home and step forward to identify him." I hesitated. "Now I think of it, none of the other victims that were killed in the same manner were married either, were they?"

That gave Mr. Keats pause. He looked fully up at me, his brow furrowing. "You were near enough to look at the body?"

"Well, yes," I said. "I thought perhaps someone had been injured, and wished to help."

Mr. Keats appeared none too pleased. "Miss Victoria, I realize you developed a keen eye for details following the death of your husband, and even managed to uncover the truth behind his murder. But you really must be careful, in future. What if this man's killer had been back there still? What if that young woman had only narrowly escaped?"

"Well then, Mr. Holmstead would have been in danger as well," I said. "As I followed him into the clearing, after all."

"Holmstead was immediately on the scene?" Mr. Keats asked. "How interesting."

I shrugged. "I am not sure there is anything interesting about his presence. After all, my own was something of an odd coincidence, as well."

"Quite so," he said, though I noticed that he still wrote the detail into his little book.

"Do you believe these deaths that have all occurred in the same fashion are connected somehow?" I asked. "That all the victims shared the same killer? Or is it possible other murderers are simply imitating the first?"

"None of that is certain at this time," Mr. Keats said. "And I apologize, Miss Victoria, but I am unable to make any further comments, as it is a police matter."

"I see," I said, sitting back further against the bench, and resuming my back and forth pushing of the carriage. Daniel, thankfully, was still napping peacefully.

Mr. Keats studied my face for a few moments, his eyes narrowing slightly.

"I received your letter," he said, removing his top hat. "My apologies for not having the opportunity to reply to it quite yet. I would indeed like to set up a time to meet with you to further discuss your husband's case."

"Very good," I said. "When would you be free?"

"This evening," he said. "Would that be all right?"

"Indeed," I said. "Why don't you come to the house for dinner? Say, around seven?"

"I would be happy to," he said. "In the meantime, Miss Victoria, I shall pass on your witness account to the police. Feel free to be on your way."

"Of course, Mr. Keats," I said, unsure whether he was being generous or simply wishing us out from under foot. "See you for dinner at seven."

Perhaps then I'll be able to discover exactly what you are not telling me.

"I do not understand why you are so flustered, madam. It is only dinner."

I glared up at Mrs. Bell's reflection in the mirror of my dressing table. *Simple enough for her to say. She does not have to sit through the meal with him, wondering and waiting for information she may never be able to learn.*

I had spent the majority of the afternoon worrying over my coming meeting with Mr. Keats. I was well aware that I had been the one to initiate said meeting, in hopes of learning more information about Duncan's death than what the inquirer had communicated in the letter he'd written.

Even still, I found myself concerned over whether or not he had been able to find anything in the first place.

"I know what you are thinking," Mrs. Bell said as she set another of my curls in place with a silver pin. My maid had recently turned in her notice and left to get married, leaving the housekeeper to perform such tasks for me.

"Do you now?" I asked, smiling at her through the mirror. "That's quite a risky statement."

Mrs. Bell gave me a flat look that would have sent me running from the room had I still been a child. "You worry that he has no new information about the late master's death," she said. "And that is a perfectly reasonable concern. But what you must realize is if that is the truth, then there is nothing to be done about it. You have done what you could, and you may just have to accept that we may never know who encouraged the killer's actions."

I frowned up at her. "But there has to be an answer, somewhere..." I said.

"It is natural to be worried for your own safety and for that of the little master," Mrs. Bell said as she loosened another dark curl from a roller, letting it unwind slowly. "But I truly do think that if anyone had meant harm to you in any way, they would have made their move already. Wouldn't you agree?" she asked.

I huffed. "Yes, the same thought has crossed my mind as well," I admitted.

The truth was I simply hated the thought that what happened to Duncan could have been so random, and that Adam could have developed such a mad scheme entirely on his own. And I feared that if there was more to it all than met the eye, then I would never know exactly what caused someone to hate my husband so much they wanted him dead.

But Mrs. Bell was correct that I could do nothing about any of that in this moment, so I tried to set it all from my mind for a little while.

She helped me to dress in a dinner gown that I had worn while Duncan was courting me. One of my mother's, it was a deep shade of violet, and the gloves that matched fit me as perfectly as they had once fit her. Being a man, Mr. Keats could not be expected to know that everything I wore, though respectably elegant, was rather tired and out of style this season. At least, I hoped he would not notice. My diminished clothing allowance was not something I was eager to advertise.

Mrs. Bell made a passing comment about how much effort I was putting in for a dinner that was supposed to be nothing more than business, but I dismissed it. "If I do not put in the effort, then how is he to take me seriously?"

"He is well aware of your station," Mrs. Bell reminded me.

"Is he, though?" I asked. "Certainly he knows my in-laws, but does he realize what an important man my father was?"

Even as I asked the question, I knew it was a foolish one. A man in Mr. Keats's profession would undoubtedly have gathered all the relevant information about everyone he did business with. More than likely, the detective knew far more about my background than I did his.

I thought with some dissatisfaction that this put me at a disadvantage.

It was just before seven in the evening when I kissed Daniel on the forehead, leaving him with his nanny in his new nursery. Shortly after Duncan's death, I had insisted that the servants move the nursery down the hall closer to my room. They had cleaned out Duncan's old room, and after changing the wallpaper from the dreary, dark color it was, and opening the windows to air out the place, I was much happier with Daniel's location in the middle of the night.

I had waited for Duncan's disappearance to hit me, to grieve me...but it never did. If anything, the relief grew with each passing day, and I found myself grateful for his absence. The constant worry I used to experience before falling asleep at night had disappeared, and for the first time since Daniel was born, I felt comfortable in my own home.

It did not change the fact that I still adamantly wanted to know who it was that shared responsibility with my lunatic footman for the loss of Duncan's life. I had always known that London had a deep, dark underground where shady deals happened and people lost their lives, but I never expected it would end up crossing my path like it had.

"Now, you be good for Eliza," I said, passing the squirming baby to his nurse. "Your mama is just going to have dinner with the nice inquirer."

"You look lovely, madam," Eliza said. "I imagine Mr. Keats will think so as well."

I lifted a brow. "And why should Mr. Keats have an opinion one way or another?" I asked.

Eliza shrank in on herself. "Oh, I just...the way he looked at you this morning – "

"I would be careful what you say, Eliza," I said firmly. "Mr. Keats may have the manners of a gentleman but I doubt very much that he was born into any lofty station. Let us not forget he was employed by the Sedgewick family."

"Yes, of course, madam," Eliza said with a quick nod.

A quiet voice in the back of my mind reminded me that my own circumstances were increasingly precarious. Was I not being driven to seek work for my income? I was hardly in any position to look down my nose at Mr. Keats's uncertain social standing. Still, it was difficult to erase the habits of a lifetime.

"Madam, it is nearly seven," came Mrs. Bell's voice.

I looked at Eliza. "If the baby becomes inconsolable

by the time he needs to be fed again, do not worry about interrupting our meeting. I don't imagine it will take very long."

I made my way downstairs a few moments later, and took my place beside Warrington, who was waiting near the front door.

"You look lovely this evening, madam, if I may say so," the butler said, inclining his head.

Before I could respond, there came a knock at the door.

Warrington pulled the door open, and Mr. Keats stood on the other side. He wore a suit of deep grey now, with a polished pair of shoes and his usual black top hat with the white ribbon wrapped around it.

He stood casually on the front steps, as comfortably as if he were visiting an old friend.

"Good evening, Mr. Warrington," he said with a smile. "I hope I am not too early."

"Right on time, sir," Warrington said, stepping aside.

Mr. Keats walked through the door, removing his hat.

"Ah, Miss Victoria," he said, his eyes falling on me. "How kind of you to greet me at the door."

"Good evening, Mr. Keats," I said. "I trust you are well?"

"Quite well, yes, thank you," he said. "It is a relief to be able to enjoy some sustenance this evening. I have not eaten a thing since meeting my father for tea before I was called to Hyde Park this morning."

"How fortunate that my cook has prepared a delicious meal, then," I said. "If you would follow me..."

I turned and started down the hall toward the dining room.

Mr. Tulson was waiting inside for us, as was Mrs. Bell.

"This is an elegant room," Mr. Keats said. "Well decorated. Do I sense some Grecian influences?"

As Mr. Tulson helped me push in my chair, a twinge of annoyance ran down my back. It made the smile already on my face grow tighter. *How does this man seem to know something about everything?* "Indeed. Quite the eye you have."

"Would you care for port, sir?" Mr. Tulson asked quietly.

"No, thank you," Mr. Keats said. "I would prefer tea, if I may."

"Certainly, sir," Mr. Tulson said. "And for madam?"

"Tea as well, please," I said, my eyes not leaving Mr. Keats.

My guest seemed fascinated with the artwork on the walls and the sculptures on the mantlepiece over the fireplace.

"No port, Mr. Keats?" I asked. "I have yet to meet a gentleman who doesn't enjoy a glass with dinner. My husband certainly did."

"In my profession, it is necessary to keep my senses sharp at all times. I am called away at a moment's notice, and there are many days when I leave my home before the sun rises and do not return until well after it sets," he said.

I studied him for a moment, and saw a flash of something in his clear, grey eyes.

"It sounds rather lonely, when you put it that way," I said.

He met my gaze, and whatever it was that I'd seen vanished. "Not lonely, no," he said. "I have chosen this life, and have no regrets."

"Well, I for one am thankful that you did choose it, and for your efforts in locating the killer of my husband," I said. "Without you and your influence, I never would have suspected that someone in my household could have been capable of something so horrific."

He inclined his head. "I was simply doing my job, Miss Victoria. I was pleased to do so."

"Now..." I said, shifting in my chair. "Perhaps I am overstepping my bounds, but you said in your letter that you thought you might have discerned a possible direction that would lead you to the other person who had a hand in my husband's death."

"Indeed," he said. "Though of course since I sent the letter to you my circumstances have obviously changed, and so I have had to continue the investigation on my own time."

"Pardon me," I said. "But what do you mean that your circumstances have obviously changed?"

An expression passed over his face that I had never seen there before, and it was a moment before I realized it was surprise. "Your father-in-law," he said, pausing, waiting for me to understand. "He has decided to close the case."

"He what?" I asked. "When did he do that?"

"I would have assumed that you knew," Mr. Keats said.

"Allow me to be the first to inform you that my father-in-law and I do not see eye to eye on many matters," I said.

Mr. Tulson returned with our tea, setting down the cups before us before bowing himself back out of the room and down to the kitchens for our first course.

"My apologies, Miss Victoria," Mr. Keats said. "I assumed he would have informed you."

"Did he give reason for deciding to close the case?" I asked. "Given the fact that we still do not know everything?"

"He simply believed the matter to be resolved, as he wasn't quite sure that he...well, that he truly believed your testimony of what your murderous footman had said before he died. The story about someone in a pub having convinced the footman to kill your late husband was tenuous and impossible to confirm. I suspect Mr. Sedgwick was also concerned about the growing expense of my investigation."

I supposed I should not have been entirely surprised by the development. I knew only too well that the continued investigation had been based more on vague suspicions than hard facts. Still, it was impossible to accept the idea of never getting to the bottom of the matter.

"I am sorry," Mr. Keats said. "Mr. Sedgewick wrote that his brother's death had been tragic enough and the family could endure no further – "

"The letter was from Hudson?" I interrupted.

"Yes," Mr. Keats said. "On behalf of your father-in-law. He said his father was under the weather but had instructed him to write."

"I see," I said, taking no trouble to hide my disappointment.

"I wish you to know, however, that I do not abandon an investigation until *I* am satisfied I have all the answers," Mr. Keats continued. "And I am not satisfied, in this instance. I do believe there is still more to your husband's death than what meets the eye."

"But you are no longer being paid for your work," I pointed out.

"That is true," Mr. Keats said. "But it does not change the fact that the case remains open in my mind, even if only a sliver. I wish to know the truth, and will do my best to continue the investigation when I am able."

I sighed heavily, shaking my head. "I do not wish you to do so without pay," I said. "But unfortunately, my financial circumstances are such that I can offer nothing."

Mr. Tulson appeared at that moment, and I was grateful for the interruption, as I had a great deal of disappointing information to absorb.

He set down bowls of a cream soup before us, garnished with toasted pumpkin seeds.

We sat in silence for a few minutes as we began to eat, and I thought over what Mr. Keats had said.

My in-laws believe the matter to be handled. Why can I not accept such a possibility? Why do I feel compelled to keep digging for more answers, when there may never be enough to satisfy me?

"Mr. Keats," I said as I set my spoon down beside my half-finished bowl. "I must thank you for continuing to look for my husband's killer, regardless of payment."

"Certainly," he said. "I can understand your desire to learn the full truth about his death. You must miss him dearly."

I swallowed, and in a strange moment of inexplicable trust, I said, "Do not misunderstand me, Mr. Keats. My marriage was not a happy one, nor can I honestly say my husband was a particularly excellent man. You must have discerned as much during your investigation."

It felt unexpectedly comforting to get the truth out into the open like that. I did not give Mr. Keats a chance to respond, before hurrying on. "My concern with locating Duncan's killer has far less to do with him, and far more to do with protecting myself and my son. Also, I wish to have a full answer for little Daniel one day, when he is old enough to ask what happened to his father."

If Mr. Keats found anything I said a shocking revelation, his unchanging expression did not show it. I had the sense that he was a difficult man to surprise.

"I am sorry if you think rather less of me now," I said. "I imagine you don't hear every day that the victim you are seeking justice for is not greatly mourned."

"You might be surprised about some of the cases I have been hired to look into in the past..." Mr. Keats said.

Mr. Tulson appeared with our second course, a fragrant roasted pheasant, which had been paired with a thick, rich gravy and boiled potatoes.

It seemed like a good time to change the subject.

"I confess, Mr. Keats, I am quite curious about one case that you have taken on," I said. "The one involving the deaths that have been occurring in Hyde Park recently."

The detective averted his gaze as he began to eat. "Indeed," he said. "It has been most interesting."

"And to be asked by Scotland Yard for your help," I said, slicing a piece of the pheasant with my knife. "I knew you were well respected in the city, but to see you recognized by the police themselves shows how far your reputation precedes you."

"Yes, I suppose it does," Mr. Keats said.

My eyes narrowed as I looked down the table at him. *Suddenly quiet now, are we, Mr. Keats?* "I imagine you cannot discuss the case at great length, given the severity of the matter..." I began. "But I was consumed with thoughts of it all day, as you can imagine, having witnessed such an atrocity. Do you believe this to be the work of one killer? And what sort of motive might he have?"

"I apologize, Miss Victoria, but as you say, I am not at liberty to speak about the case," he said. "As it is a police matter, I have been asked to keep quiet about it until the investigation is resolved. I am certain you understand."

I tried to conceal my annoyance. *Did I not just share my feelings with this man about Duncan, thoughts that might prove complicated for me if they were to be made public? The very least he could do is give me the slightest hint, the smallest piece of information I might be able to use for my own investigations.*

"What of the unfortunate victim?" I asked. "Have you discovered his identity by now?"

"We are still not certain of his name yet," Mr. Keats said. "I spent the majority of the day questioning bystanders, while others cleaned up the scene and set the park back in order. I had just enough time to go home and change before coming here. I have barely had a moment to breathe."

It was clear I would not get any further information out of him that evening. No name, no motive, no possible theories.

"Well," I said, smiling tightly at him. "I do hope that you will take this evening to rest then, Mr. Keats. Eat your fill, and know that you are in good hands."

"Your kindness is great, Miss Victoria," he said, and continued to happily eat the food before him.

I watched him for a moment, and then frowned.

I will get that information...somehow. I must know what happened in Hyde Park.

7

I should not have been surprised that Mr. Keats would not share information with me about his business, or about the deaths occurring in the city. I had hoped he might tell me more about how he managed to be invited onto official cases like this one, acquiring the attention, and presumably the funds, of Scotland Yard.

How had he begun his career? What sort of investigations did he have to take on before being asked to investigate murders like the white dove feather case?

"Well, the only way I am going to be able to look into this matter myself is by starting at the very bottom and working my way up," I said the next morning at breakfast. The skies outside the tall windows, dark and grey, held promise of rain as the clouds swelled. "First and foremost, I must learn who this newest victim was.

And perhaps more importantly, who he might have been related to."

Mrs. Bell looked disappointed with my level of enthusiasm on the subject. She seemed far more interested in hearing my thoughts about dinner last night with Mr. Keats.

"He is quite a pleasant gentleman, do you not think?" Mrs. Bell asked, setting my tea down in front of me. "Handsome, well connected, and respected."

"Why, Mrs. Bell..." I said, lifting an eyebrow. "I believe you are becoming infatuated with our Mr. Keats."

My housekeeper huffed, her cheeks coloring. "Madam, I was merely suggesting – "

"I understand perfectly well what you were suggesting," I said mildly. "And I am surprised at you, Mrs. Bell. From the nanny and other servants, I would expect this sort of thing, but you are surely aware that a good looking man is the last thought on my mind these days. Even if it were otherwise, Mr. Branwell Keats and I would hardly be a suitable match."

"If you say so, madam," Mrs. Bell muttered, which I knew was as close as the woman would come to arguing with me.

Warrington came into the dining room a short time later, carrying the post. "The paper, and some letters for you, madam," he said, setting them down before me. "Including one from your cousin."

"How kind of her," I said, pushing the letters aside. "I shall read it later. For now, I wish to see if – yes, this is exactly what I wanted to see."

Unfolding the newspaper, I searched the front page for only a moment before I discovered what I was looking for.

"Yes," I said, setting the paper down and prodding the photograph on the front page. "This is the man whose body was found in the park yesterday. I am certain of it."

It was rather sad to see the victim's photograph in the paper after seeing how horror-stricken his face had been the day before. In life, he had certainly looked better.

"He looks so peaceful here," I said, studying the man's face. "Entirely unaware of the awful fate that will one day await him."

"Madam..." Mrs. Bell said. "Surely you need not dwell on such dark things?"

I ignored her chiding.

The man was in his mid-thirties, it seemed. Named Mr. Franklin Dullard, he was a professor of law at the local university, and also had several published works that had evidently been well received.

"*A shrewd thinker, Mr. Dullard was feared by his students and well respected by his peers. He held a seat in the university's council, and everyone who met him remem-*

bers him as one of the most brilliant men they ever had the pleasure of knowing," I read.

I lowered the paper and stared ahead, chewing on the inside of my lip.

"What on earth could this man possibly have in common with the last victim?" I asked.

I stared down at his photograph. He was entirely different from...what was the other fellow's name? Mr. Locke? Where Mr. Locke had a broad face with deep-set eyes, Mr. Dullard was a svelte sort of man with a narrow jaw and large eyes that reminded me vaguely of an owl.

"They look nothing alike," I said. "Though I suppose that matters little. One probably does not choose to murder people based solely on their appearance."

"If this is indeed the act of one killer, there must be a reason behind it," Mrs. Bell said with a shudder. "Something that ties them together."

"One would certainly think so," Warrington said with a frown. "But there is no guarantee. If this is the work of a madman, then the deaths could truly be random. And the more random they are, the harder it will be for the authorities to find the murderer."

"Mr. Locke was an accountant, was he not?" I asked. "And Mr. Dullard here was a professor."

"The only connection I see between any of them is that they were all unmarried at the time, or widowed, and they all were found in Hyde Park," Warrington said.

"That is not a great deal to go on, is it?" I asked, chewing my lip once more.

"Four deaths..." Mrs. Bell said. "And no sign of them stopping. What if they discover yet another body today? Madam, I beg you to steer clear of that park until all of this is resolved."

"But all of the victims seem to be men," I said. "I should be perfectly safe."

"There is no predicting the actions of a lunatic," Mrs. Bell said. "How can you be certain he will not begin targeting female victims next? And think of the little master. You would not wish to put little Daniel in harm's way."

I pursed my lips. "No, of course not," I said. "I would never. However...what if someone comes to me, asking for help?" I flipped the page of the newspaper over and indicated my own advertisement. "With all of these deaths, people are going to be frightened and desperate."

"They already are frightened," Warrington said. "The police are involved. This case just became a great deal more important in the eyes of Scotland Yard. They are not going to take it lightly. That means it is likely going to be that much more difficult to resolve, if they haven't been able to pin down the killer yet."

"With Mr. Keats working on the case, they will find the murderer," I said.

"You have confidence in him, madam?" Mrs. Bell asked.

I shrugged my shoulders. "He was the one who tipped me off that it could have been one of my staff that killed Duncan," I said. "Though in the end, I believe I could have figured it out on my own, his suggestion did cause me to focus my suspicions on the culprit. Clearly, his intuition was reliable."

I looked back down at the paper. "What strikes me is that it is almost as if the killer wishes the bodies to be found," I said. "Leaving them in Hyde Park, out in the open? Why would they risk exposing themselves?"

Mrs. Bell suddenly looked rather green. "That is an even more troubling thought, is it not? They care so little for the lives of those they kill that they choose to display them so openly?"

"It's troubling because it is as if they have no fear of being caught," Warrington said. "As if they are saying to the world that they have already outwitted the authorities and gotten away with it, so what prevents them from doing so again?"

I shuddered. "That is odd..."

I found myself fascinated, and yet horrified at the same time, by the whole matter.

"How could anyone kill so easily? And so many times?" I asked.

I looked back down at the paper, and saw there was a continuation of the article on the next page. I flipped it over and found a picture of a younger man, dressed in a naval officer's uniform.

Commander Townsend's killer has yet to be found, and his loved ones and friends are beginning to wonder if these deaths are all connected somehow. The Commander's friend and colleague, Lieutenant Commander William Wright, spoke with our editor, and had a message for anyone who might have more information.

"If anyone out there has any further information regarding the death of Commander Townsend, I would ask you to come forward with it. Speak with the police, or speak with the private inquirer involved in the case. Our families are grieving, and we do not wish to see anyone else have to suffer through the same pain. If anyone knows anything, anything at all, we ask that they step forward with courage and help put an end to this madness."

This Lieutenant Commander Wright...was it possible that he could shed more light on the situation for me?

"Would it be wise to speak with this man?" I wondered aloud. "I could garner further information about the victims. Perhaps with enough information about them, I can put all of the pieces of this puzzle together and discern what it is that connects them?"

"It surely seems wise to gather as much informa-tion as possible, madam," Warrington said. "Though one must wonder...what if there is nothing connecting these men?"

"And if the killer strikes again, it will simply make the whole matter harder to unravel," Mrs. Bell said. "More details, more differences. The more deaths that occur, the killer is just that much harder to trace."

"That, and this poor family may think you are coming forward with the information they so desperately want," Warrington said.

"Perhaps," I said. "But it may also be that by speaking with them, I might find the killer, and therefore give them that information. What if no one has gone to see them, since the murder might have seemed random at the time? Of course the police will be investigating the most recent victims...but what if details about the Commander's death go unnoticed before it is too late? This could be a lead that I uncover first. And who knows? Perhaps it will end up being the most important information in the end."

"Might I make a suggestion, madam?" Warrington asked.

"Of course," I said.

"If you decide to go through with your plan, perhaps I might accompany you? Having retired from the military myself, I shall know how to speak with the person you intend to interview, and my presence might provide protection, should it be needed."

"It is a sensible idea," I agreed. "I shall write to

inquire after a time when I might visit, and then, we shall get to the bottom of this."

And so begins my first real investigation... It certainly hasn't happened the way I had expected, but I will make the most of it.

Take care, Mr. Keats, for I may very well resolve this string of murders before you do.

8

I t took no time to compile a letter that I was satisfied with to send over to the Lieutenant Commander Wright. Taking great care to ensure there was no misunderstanding about my desire to speak with him, I made it clear from the very beginning that I was looking for information.

Dear Lieutenant Commander Wright,

I hope this letter finds you well, and I do hope you will pardon the suddenness of it. My name is Victoria Ward, and I am a private inquirer. I recently saw your testimonial in the newspaper, and wished to reach out to you. It must be quite troubling that the Commander's killer has yet to be found, but with the newest string of murders occurring across London, I and very likely many others desire to get to the bottom of all this and ensure those who are involved are punished accordingly.

I am writing to you to offer my services. While other detectives are investigating the most recent deaths, I have reason to believe that Commander Townsend's death is connected somehow. I should like to come and speak with you at your earliest convenience, in order to perhaps garner further information about the Commander and his life, as I believe you may very well be the best chance we have at finding this killer.

I await your response, and humbly ask that you take my offer into consideration. I shall not disappoint you.

I signed it and sent it on its way, hopeful for a return.

A return came indeed, less than a week later.

We agreed upon a time to meet.

It was the 15th of September when Warrington and I sat together in a hansom cab, less than a quarter of a mile away from the Lieutenant Commander's home, when the horse hastened to a sudden stop, causing our driver to cry out in alarm.

"For goodness sake, what could be the cause of this delay?" I asked, righting my hat and adjusting the ribbon beneath my chin.

Warrington peered around us, squinting into the bright afternoon sun. "Good heavens, there appears to be quite the crowd here."

"A crowd?" I asked. "For what reason?"

"They seem to be gathered outside that home,"

Warrington said. "What number did you say the Lieutenant Commander lived at, madam?"

"Number four hundred and three," I said, shifting in my seat so that I, too, could look around the side of the cab

"That is what I thought," Warrington said. "I fear these people are members of the press, reporters for the newspapers."

My stomach twisted into knots. "But why are they here now of all times?"

The cab driver raised his voice. "Sorry, Miss, but we cannot make it past," he said. "The crowd is too thick."

I sighed. "Very well," I said.

Warrington helped me safely down onto the street and went to pay the driver, as I walked around to stare up at the row house across the street where the people were all gathered.

"They certainly are reporters," I said, glowering at a photographer with a large camera set up on a stand, as well as those people with pads of paper in their hands, ready and eager to begin writing. "The question is what are they doing here?"

"From the looks of them, they've been here for several hours," Warrington said, coming around to stand with me.

"How can you tell that?" I asked.

"From the exhaustion in their faces, madam," Warrington said.

I looked closer, noting how a young man in a green suit leaned against his camera stand. And how a woman with untidy hair paced slowly, with an air of boredom, back and forth across the sidewalk. Warrington was right. Something told me they had been here for some time, waiting to see the Lieutenant Commander as well.

A shiver of excitement raced down my spine, but the annoyance I felt outweighed it.

"We shall enter as we normally would," I decided. "But not without caution. Come, Warrington."

I gathered up my skirts and marched across the street as soon as the coast was clear.

Warrington and I attracted the gaze of a few of the reporters on the outskirts of the group, perhaps interested in some sort of movement apart from the others nearby.

My stepping up onto the sidewalk in front of the home seemed to bring the rest of them to life. At once, there were shouts and cries from the crowd, all vying for our attention.

"Miss, Miss! Are you related to the Wrights?" came the voice of a middle-aged man with a bald spot that left very little hair around the rest of his head.

"Do you know what happened to Commander Townsend?" asked another man.

"Do you have any comments for the people of

London on behalf of the Lieutenant Commander?" asked a young man with a slight stutter in his words.

I found myself attempting to listen to all of their questions, their voices carrying over one another, growing in volume, all trying desperately to get my attention.

My confidence slipped, under the onslaught. I could only stand there in stunned silence, uncertain where to begin. *No, of course I am not related – how could I know what happened to – I haven't even met the man yet!*

Warrington murmured in my ear. "We must not be late for our appointment with the Lieutenant Commander, madam."

The sound of his voice, though quieter than the others, was enough to bring me back to myself.

"Of course," I said. "Yes, you are right. Let us go in."

As I walked toward the steps, the mob of reporters seemed to move as one toward me, keeping the close distance between us. Their shouting, too, grew louder.

"Miss, Miss, why has the Lieutenant Commander been so afraid to answer questions when he so clearly stated that he was looking for information?" asked another man with a hard frown that seemed to be his permanent expression.

With you lot out here, it's no wonder he decided to stay inside...

Warrington stepped between us, thanking them and nodding as we headed up the stairs.

I knocked on the door, very aware of the many eyes fixed on my back. Their frantic questions ceased, and they waited with what seemed to be baited breath.

It was only a few moments before the door was pulled open, and the face of a very short woman appeared in the doorway, a small black hat fixed atop her snowy white hair

"Are you Miss Ward?" she asked in a low voice, keeping back from the crack she'd opened in the door.

Still unaccustomed to the name, it took me several seconds to recall that Miss Ward was indeed me, as far as my investigative work was concerned.

"Yes, I am she," I said, glancing briefly over my shoulder at the reporters. I half expected some of them to charge the steps and bolt in through the front door while they had the chance. For now, however, they seemed more like watchful dogs, waiting to see what we might do next.

"Then please, come in," the woman said.

She stepped aside and Warrington and I slipped inside. No sooner were Warrington's coattails over the threshold than she slammed the door shut, locking it tight.

She breathed a sigh of relief as she turned around to us.

An older woman who stood almost to my shoulder, she was clearly the housekeeper, judging by the way she carried herself. Her hair was pulled back in a tight bun at the nape of her neck, and her face seemed to carry the echo of a very pretty woman, with high cheekbones and stunningly blue eyes.

"My apologies," she said. "But those reporters have been nothing but a nuisance for days now. Ever since the Lieutenant Commander's plea for help was posted in the papers, they have been like vultures outside the front door. The poor man does not feel comfortable stepping outside the house, as he is bombarded the moment he does."

"And the police will not do anything?" I asked.

"The police are very nearly as bad," the woman said. "They do not seem to care how badly the reporters are disturbing us, only that the Lieutenant Commander might have information about Commander Townsend."

I winced. "I do apologize, then, for our addition to all of the questions," I said. "I can imagine the Lieutenant Commander is fed up with all of the attention."

"Indeed he certainly is," the woman said. "As is his wife. However...they are quite pleased to receive you, Miss Ward. The last detective hired for this investigation quit on the Commander's family very early in, and no answer was ever given as to why. Lieutenant Commander Wright believes that you may be the answer to his prayers."

"Well, I certainly hope to be of help," I said.

"Please forgive my manners," the woman said

suddenly, laying a hand over her heart. "My name is Mrs. Barton. I am the Lieutenant Commander's housekeeper."

"A pleasure to meet you, Mrs. Barton. This is my... assistant, Mr. Warrington."

I was unsure whether this Miss Ward character I now played was the sort of woman who would have a butler, so it seemed best to keep Warrington's role vague.

Mrs. Barton said, "Well, come along please. Right this way."

She gestured for us to follow her from the lavishly decorated foyer, complete with a large portrait of a handsome family with three young children, all of whom had dark, straight hair.

"I hope you do not mind, the Lieutenant Commander has ordered tea in his study today while his wife and children are out. He thought it best to discuss the Commander's death without any curious little ears listening in," Mrs. Barton said as we continued through the house.

It was a comfortable looking home, not overly large, but very clean and well decorated. It seemed that the Lieutenant Commander's wife was rather fond of French furnishings, and I caught a glimpse of some pottery painted with pale blues and yellows that I knew were of French origin.

"I understand entirely," I said. "I have a son as well. He is very nearly six months old now."

"So young," Mrs. Barton said. "How lovely. Here we are."

She turned down a narrow hall lined with portraits and plush green carpeting, very near the back of the rowhouse. She stopped just beyond and gestured inside a door off to the left.

"Sir, Miss Ward is here to see you," she said.

"Send her in," said a man's voice.

Warrington and I stepped through the doorway into an elegant study. The walls, all lined with deep, rich mahogany wood, were nearly obscured due to the swollen, overstuffed bookshelves that lined each wall. A fireplace stood in the far corner, though the hearth was dark and cold. The windows behind the desk were standing open, and the sounds of the city poured inside.

The man seated at the desk was much the sort I expected to find, though a little younger. Perhaps in his late thirties or early forties, he had a large build. His short beard was the same nutty brown color as the hair he wore trimmed close to his head. He sat with his shoulders and back ramrod straight, and yet was still writing a letter with immense precision.

He looked up as we entered, and set down his pen. "Yes, welcome, Miss Ward. It is good to finally meet you in person."

He rose from his seat and gestured to the two leather armchairs across from his desk.

"Likewise, Lieutenant Commander," I said.

As we approached, he held out his hand, which I shook.

"This is Mr. Warrington, who assists me," I said.

"A pleasure to meet you, Mr. Warrington," the Lieutenant Commander said. "You look somewhat familiar to me."

"I thought the very same thing, sir," Mrs. Barton said, lingering near the door.

"Warrington was in the military for twenty years," I said, smiling over at him.

"Were you now?" the Lieutenant Commander asked. "Twenty years...and now retired?"

Warrington nodded. "Yes, sir."

"Well, the military is not an easy sort of life, is it?" the Lieutenant Commander asked. He looked up at Mrs. Barton. "Would you be so kind as to pour tea for our guests?"

Mrs. Barton nodded and scurried to the other side of the room, where a low buffet table held a steaming silver teapot and several more French floral cups.

"Now, I confess I was rather surprised to receive your letter," the Lieutenant Commander said. "The plea I had put out in the newspaper received a much greater response than I had imagined it would."

"Hence the crowd gathered outside," I said.

He nodded. "They have been quite the nuisance. I told them when they first arrived that I was looking for information, not to provide answers. For how can I provide answers to questions that I do not know, and am asking myself?"

I shook my head. "Like hungry lions they are, waiting for their next kill."

"Precisely," he said. "So, what can I do to help you? I am happy, of course, to answer any questions I am able."

"Well, Lieutenant Commander, as I said in my letter, I believe that Commander Townsend's death may very well be connected with the other more recent murders that have occurred," I said. "I would be interested in knowing more about the Commander, as well as the events leading up to his death."

The Lieutenant Commander's hard exterior seemed to falter for but a moment. He regarded the top of his handsomely polished desk with great interest, his brow furrowing. "Commander Townsend..." he began. "He was an excellent man. A dear friend, and like a brother to me. He saved my life more than once, you know. His family and mine were very close; his sister and my wife are dear friends, and my children had come to call him their uncle..."

I looked sidelong over at Warrington, who seemed to be keenly focused on the Lieutenant Commander's words.

"He sounds like an upstanding man," I said.

"Oh, yes," the Lieutenant Commander said with a firm nod. "Quite so. Perhaps the most honorable I ever served alongside."

"Do you know of anyone who might have wished him harm?" I asked. "Any enemies that he might have had?"

The Lieutenant Commander shook his head. "No, not any at all. Even during our time in the service together, everyone respected him and his ways of handling situations. I was humbled to have the opportunity to act as his Lieutenant Commander."

"But a man of such standing had to have more than a few enemies in high places," I said. "Surely there must have been someone who would have wanted him gone? Perhaps for his position? Or out of sheer jealousy?"

"I suppose it is possible, but no one like that comes to mind," the Lieutenant Commander said. "I wish I could think of any enemy he had. It might have made the initial investigation that much easier."

I nodded, pursing my lips as Mrs. Barton returned with hot cups of tea for Warrington and I. "Cream or sugar?" she asked, setting the cups down before us.

"Yes, please," I said.

She hurried back over to the buffet.

"How old was the Commander when he was killed?" I asked.

"Thirty-eight, I believe," the Lieutenant Commander said. "Not a great deal older than myself."

"How about any lovers?" I asked. "Did he have any sort of falling out with a woman before he died?"

"No," the Lieutenant Commander said. "To be honest, I think he planned to propose to a young lady he had been seeing. She has been investigated by the police, however, and has since moved out of London."

"Are you certain they had no squabbles before his death?" I asked.

The Lieutenant Commander shook his head. "No, they certainly had not. I think this was all a great shock to her."

"She could have been lying," I said. "Perhaps you should give me her name."

"It was not her," the Lieutenant Commander said firmly. "I assure you. I may not be a detective, Miss Ward, but I do have an understanding of people and which of them are capable of deception. She was not. She loved Commander Townsend. She was devastated when they found him dead."

"Very well," I said, still having reservations. "What happened leading up to his death?"

Mrs. Barton set the cream and sugar bowls down before us.

"I am not entirely aware of all the specifics," the Lieutenant Commander said. "He and I had attended a meeting together three days before hand, where the

Commander had been given the task of leading basic training for new recruits this coming autumn. He was eager to do so. Afterwards, the last time I saw him was the next night when my wife and I had him over for dinner." Hard lines appeared in his face, and he couldn't meet my eye. "He died the following night... and they found him in the morning alongside the edge of the pond in the middle of Hyde Park."

"Life seemed ordinary for him," I said. "When he was visiting you for dinner, did anything appear unusual?"

"No, not at all," the Lieutenant Commander said. "That is what is so bizarre about it all. No matter how much I think about it, go over it in my own mind, I cannot seem to pinpoint an exact moment where something might have occurred. Nothing, even now, seemed strange enough that it could have been the reason that he died."

"Did he live alone?" I asked.

"Yes," he said. "Which is rather unfortunate. I wish someone might have seen him shortly before he died, but there were no witnesses even then, and I doubt there would be any now."

It wasn't long before Warrington and I were thanking the Lieutenant Commander for his time, leaving with our cups of tea only half finished.

"You have my word, Lieutenant Commander," I said. "I will do everything in my power to find whoever it was that killed Commander Townsend. They will be brought to justice, if I have anything to say about it."

"I am glad to hear it, Miss Ward," he said. "I must say I am desperate to put this all behind us, and I wish that I could have given you more of the information you were looking for."

"It's quite all right," I said. "I am truly sorry for the loss of your friend."

He gave me a smile, tinged with sadness.

Warrington and I called a hansom cab over, and began our journey back home.

"Who could have killed a man like that, Warrington?" I asked. "It utterly baffles me."

"And I, madam..." Warrington said. "A man of such prestige and honor, the sort without enemies. It is difficult to imagine why he should have ended up dead, unless someone in his life was entirely too jealous."

"You think it might have been a personal quarrel then?" I asked. "But what of the other murders?"

"That is the troubling part, isn't it?" Warrington asked. "A killer whose motive is impossible to read..."

What sort of case have I gotten myself into?

9

Commander Townsend was on my mind for the next few days. Part of me struggled with the idea that he was truly such an upstanding man. Surely there had to have been *something* in his life, a secret he would have wanted kept, that would have drawn the attention of some unsavory folk. It had to have been the same with all the men who were killed, surely?

"Madam, one does not have to be entangled in something dreadful or secret in order to be murdered," Mrs. Bell said to me as we perused the vegetable stand at the farmer's market that following Saturday. "It is quite possible that the killer was nothing more than a madman who had nothing better to do."

"But something has to tie them all together," I said as she loaded bundles of herbs and freshly picked carrots into a basket hanging in the crook of her arm. It was not typical for me to accompany her on such an errand, but I had felt restless and in need of an excuse to escape the gloomy house for awhile.

"It all seems too deliberate," I continued. "Why choose random victims, but kill them all in the same way? It appears far too carefully planned. And the killer always seems to be one step ahead of everyone."

The woman behind the stand at the farmer's market looked up as Mrs. Bell began to paw through the turnips. "Are you talking about the Hyde Park murders?" she asked in her Cockney accent.

"Yes, we are," I said.

"Horrible stuff that is," she said, her eyes widening. "But from what I've heard, the killer was caught!"

"Caught?" both Mrs. Bell and I asked at the same time.

"Indeed," said the woman with a fervent nod. "Just heard a newsboy shouting about it. A special edition of the paper, it seems."

"But how?" I asked. "The killer has been eluding them for months. How could they have suddenly found him?"

The woman shrugged. "Dunno. But it's mighty good news, if you ask me. Too many people were afraid to come down here near the Park, wondering if they might get snatched up and have their hearts ripped out."

I stared around, searching for the newsboy she spoke of, who might still be lingering nearby.

"Thank you for your produce," Mrs. Bell said, pressing some coins into the woman's hand.

I was already on the move.

The lad wasn't difficult to locate; I heard him before I saw him. He stood on the street corner nearest the bakery and the grocer, waving a fresh stack of papers in the air. "Hyde Park Murderer caught!" he shouted. "Scotland Yard promises peace at last!"

I frowned. "We'll see about that..." I said.

I went over to the boy and bought a paper before hurrying back to the lamppost where Mrs. Bell waited.

I fumbled with the paper for a moment as a gust of wind swept up the street, but quickly managed to unfold it, staring at the article on the front.

Hyde Park Murderer Found! Scotland Yard Urges Public to Remain Calm!

Special Report

On the evening of September the 19th, at precisely ten o'clock, the killer now known as the Hyde Park Murderer was caught in the act of leaving a body in an alleyway just outside of the park.

The victim, a one Mr. Ronald Quill, was killed in much the same way the others had been before him. The fatal wound was declared to be a stabbing in the heart, as well as one across the abdomen. It seemed the killer was going to leave his signature behind, as well, for Constable Williams

– the man who spotted the killer – found a white pigeon feather in the killer's pocket.

Mr. Ronald Quill was a stockyard worker, who seemed to have some sort of past dealings with the killer – at least according to one account. He is survived by his wife and four sons.

The killer was discovered to be a young man named Henry Roper, a dock worker who, according to authorities, simply grew weary of all the "rich folk getting away with murder" and so decided to take matters into his own hands.

He admits to having been behind the rest of the murders, as well. When asked why he committed such terrible, violent crimes, he said once again that it was all to prove that money could not save any man, and those who possessed it were just as susceptible to death as any.

Roper is now being held in police custody, while he awaits his day in court.

"This all seems far too good to be true..." I said, staring down at the page. The photograph was of Mr. Quill, who was a rather lumpy looking man with a set of eyebrows so bushy that they seemed to form one long line across his forehead.

"But what if it isn't?" Mrs. Bell asked. "Wouldn't it be a good thing if it was that simple to resolve in the end?"

"It cannot be," I said. "Not after the killer eluded capture for as long as he did."

"The authorities began to take it quite seriously

after the latest death," Mrs. Bell said. "Perhaps they realized people were becoming terrified to leave their homes."

"Yes, but there are so many questions," I said. "Look here. The first discrepancy is that the victim was stabbed in the chest, as well as the stomach. The others had chest wounds as well, but they were not simply stabbings. Their hearts had been carved from their bodies."

Mrs. Bell shuddered.

"And then there are the feathers," I went on. "The others were dove feathers, weren't they, not pigeon feathers?" I asked. "Now, Mrs. Bell, you are one of the sharpest women I know. Surely you cannot tell me that you did not notice these differences yourself..."

Her cheeks flushed scarlet. "Well, naturally I noticed them, madam," she said. "Yes, I noticed them. I also noticed he was a married man, while the other victims were not."

"Precisely," I said. "Which means that the police are wrong!"

In my excitement, I belatedly remembered to lower my voice and glanced at the passersby around us. Nobody was listening to our conversation, which was just as well, as there was no advantage to causing a stir.

"This of course means the killer is still out there on the loose, somewhere," I went on in a more casual tone. "And we surely cannot be the only ones who have noticed this."

"I do not know, madam," Mrs. Bell said, looking at the others bustling around on the street. "I imagine there will be a great many in this city who will accept that story, regardless of whether they believe it or not, purely out of a desire to be past it all."

"Even if the killer could strike again? And likely will?" I asked.

"Even then," Mrs. Bell said.

I pursed my lips and stared down at the paper in my hands. "You may very well be right," I admitted. "But that does not mean there is nothing I can do about it. I can go and see Mr. Keats. He was part of the case and working with the police, was he not? Yet his name was not mentioned in the article at all...which likely means he was not involved with the discovery of the killer. Perhaps then, he would have some insight in the matter."

I nodded to myself, as the idea grew firmer in my mind. "Yes, indeed," I said. "I wonder if he would be interested in my meeting with the Lieutenant Commander as well."

It seemed my restless energy was finally to be put to use. "Come along, Mrs. Bell," I said, suddenly brisk, tucking the newspaper beneath my arm. "Let us get ourselves home, so I can change my clothes and be on my way out again."

"Out where?" she asked.

"To go and see Mr. Branwell Keats at his office, of course," I said. "Quickly now. We do not have many hours left in the day."

~

MR. KEATS HELD an office on the second floor of a row of houses just south of Mayfair. It seemed to be a popular location for attorneys, scholars, and other studious professions.

As I walked up the wide, steep staircase to the second floor, I was surprised to find that my heart fluttered inside my chest like a cage of songbirds attempting to break free. Why was I so nervous? What was it about this meeting in particular that frightened me?

Because Mr. Keats has no idea of my involvement in the case up to this point. Who knows how he might react to it?

Not that his opinion made any difference to my determination, of course, but it might cause him to refuse to listen to my concerns. And right now, I needed him to hear me.

I stopped before a door with Mr. Keats's name written across the glass.

I reached up and knocked, and a moment later, heard the smooth voice of the man it belonged to just on the other side of the glass. "Come in."

I hesitated for only a moment before pushing the door open and stepping inside.

Mr. Keats stood on the far side of the room, at a window overlooking London's streets. His coat was absent from him, thrown carelessly over the back of his office chair. His top hat teetered rather precariously on the edge of the hat rack just beside the door.

He looked up as I entered, and straightened. "Miss Victoria," he said, his grey eyes widening. "What a surprise. To what do I owe this great pleasure?"

"Mr. Keats," I said, giving him a brief nod in greeting. I lifted the afternoon's special edition paper into the air, the article in question flashing before Mr. Keats. "I suppose you have already read this?" I asked.

His brow furrowed, and he looked from me to the paper and back again. "Indeed I have. But why are you here to see me about it?"

"I thought that would be obvious," I said. "I know as well as you do that this killer they have caught is not the one responsible for all the other murders."

Mr. Keats took the paper from me, and examined the image of Mr. Quill on the front page.

"I am quite surprised, Miss Victoria," Mr. Keats said, laying the paper down upon his desk before regarding me again.

"About what?" I asked.

"That you have come to know me as well as you have," he said, the hint of a smile tugging at the corner of his lips. "Why was your first thought to come and visit me?" he asked.

"Because I knew you were involved in the case," I said. "The authorities employed you to solve it, didn't they?"

"Indeed they did," he said, glancing at the paper. "Imagine my surprise when a constable appeared at my front door this morning, informing me that my payment would be sent over at my earliest convenience, as the case was now closed, the killer having been found."

"You do not believe it either, then," I said. "That the person they caught is the real murderer."

Mr. Keats sighed, tapping the portrait of Mr. Quill quite firmly. "I am not entirely sure I am at liberty to discuss these matters with one of my clients," he said. "However..."

"What?" I prompted, unable to completely contain my impatience.

He arched a brow as he looked at me. "I have been informed that you have also taken up the mantle of private inquirer. Is this true?"

"Yes," I said. "I have. All this business with my husband and his murder – it isn't that I do not trust you to resolve it as best you can, Mr. Keats, but it is more a matter of my father-in-law being so obstinate as to refuse me further funds – "

I stopped myself, realizing that I was rambling.

"I wished to learn the truth," I summarized. "And perhaps increase my income at the same time, so that I need not be so dependent upon the generosity of my late husband's relatives."

Mr. Keats nodded his head, walking around behind the back of his desk, his footsteps echoing around the quiet room. "A motivation that I can completely understand," he said. "I chose to become a detective for surprisingly similar reasons..."

I waited for a moment for him to continue, but all I saw was a distant look in his eyes.

"I do not believe the killer they found was the Hyde Park murderer, no," he went on. "There are too many discrepancies between this murder that occurred last night and the killings that have happened over the past several months. A fact that I have attempted to explain to the authorities already, but they refuse to listen...just as I imagine many in the city will refuse to do, until the real killer strikes again."

"Those were my thoughts precisely," I said. "The wound in the chest, as well as the new wound in the stomach? Not to mention the different kind of feather in the pocket..."

"The police seem to think those are superfluous details," Mr. Keats said. "Though why would a killer leave a dove feather, specifically a *white* dove feather, after four kills and then leave a pigeon's feather on the most recent? Whoever this person is, they are quite intentional with their actions."

"What can we do, then?" I asked. "If the authorities have convinced themselves they have captured the killer, then what can we do to change their minds?"

"I am not entirely certain," Mr. Keats said. "The worst possibility is that the killer will strike again, which seems very likely."

"We cannot just wait around until that happens," I said. "How could they be so foolish as to so easily believe this man, whoever he is? Henry Roper?"

"Oh, I do not doubt that he did indeed kill last night's victim," Mr. Keats said. "Roper is an imitator, a young man who, like all the rest of London, undoubtedly read all the gruesome details in the newspapers about the previous killings. It is not unheard of for such a person to develop an obsession with a crime, and then to mimic it out of fascination or desire for attention."

My stomach twisted in knots. "How despicable," I said.

"Indeed it is..." Mr. Keats said.

"Even if he knew he would be captured?" I asked.

He shrugged. "It is a dark world, Miss Victoria. In matters of crime, you will find that people often act unwisely or against their own interests."

"What can we do now, then?" I asked. "Should we try to find the real killer?"

"I have considered it, yes," he said.

I hesitated. "I suppose I am not the only one to think of it, but I went to see Lieutenant Commander Wright, the second victim's closest friend and second in command. I wanted more information about the victims, wondering if I could find the one thing that ties them all together."

"That is something I have been searching for, as well," Mr. Keats said. "No matter what I do, I cannot seem to find the missing link between them all. Yet there must be something. Some detail that I am missing..."

A few heartbeats passed, an uncomfortable silence settling over us as we realized the graveness of the situation that we faced.

"There is nothing to be done, then..." I said. "Except to wait?"

"No," Mr. Keats said. "We must look at the evidence we have, and make educated guesses from that."

"Perhaps it would be wise to sit down with a list of victims and do our best to locate the similarities between them," I said.

It certainly seemed as good an idea as any.

We planned for Mr. Keats to come by the house that evening, so we could further discuss the case. Time was running out, and if we were going to find this killer, we needed to move quickly.

I started for the door after agreeing upon six that evening, when Mr. Keats stopped me.

"And Miss Victoria?" he asked.

"Yes?" I said.

"While I admire your courage, I must warn you that being a detective is not as glamorous as you might believe. I realize you have seen your share of corpses but there is a great deal more danger involved. Tread carefully...and realize that you may very well be trading peace of mind for money in your pocket."

His words hung over me as I left his office.

10

"Let's see, now...this is all the information we have been able to collect on all four of the killings that have been committed by the Hyde Park murderer," Mr. Keats said leaning over the dining room table, his palms flat against the wood. "All four deaths, side by side..."

Mr. Tulson was just clearing away the last of our supper dishes as we spread out the information that I had spent most of the afternoon writing down. Mr. Keats had brought his own notes with him as well, and now he and I were pouring over the lists, the articles, the photographs, and the hand-written notes that we had accumulated in an attempt to finally put the case to rest.

"First victim," Mr. Keats said, pressing a finger to the photograph of a young man with pale, blonde hair.

"Christopher Wedley. Early twenties. Not a great deal was written about him, as his murder seemed to be the result of some sort of street fight as opposed to an orchestrated attack."

"A handsome young man," I said, frowning down at the picture. "But as you say, Mr. Keats, no one suspected it could have been a deliberate killing. At least not until Commander Townsend was found dead in the same fashion...What do we know about him?"

I pulled the article about his death toward myself. The murder had occurred before Duncan had died, so I likely had barely noticed something as trivial as the death of a young man I didn't know. There was indeed very little written.

"Hardly a thing, apart from his name and age," Mr. Keats said. "He had only one surviving family member, an aunt who was blind and nearly deaf, and seemed all too pleased that he was gone."

"I see..." I said, frowning.

Mr. Keats went on. "Then we have Commander Townsend. Respectable man, honored above many in the naval forces. Loving family, though never married. Extensive connections, including some members of Parliament. Wealthy, successful..."

"According to Lieutenant Commander Wright, he had no enemies," I said.

"That does surprise me, given his time in the service," Mr. Keats said.

He slid the picture of Commander Townsend along, as well as the notes I had compiled after the meeting I'd had with the Lieutenant Commander.

"The third victim, Mr. Arnold Locke," he said, pulling the more recent article to the forefront. "Accountant, also quite successful. Had quite the reputation in town, a part of some of the most prestigious clubs..."

"He seems to have been the sort of man who knew everyone and everything," I said.

Mr. Keats nodded as he skimmed the article. "Nothing about whether he was part of the good or the bad crowds of the upper echelon. I spoke with his parents just a few days ago, and they seemed to think everything he was involved with was above board."

"That would only make sense, wouldn't it?" I asked. "No one wishes to think their child could be involved in dark dealings, do they? Especially not after he had been so gruesomely killed."

"Fair point," Mr. Keats said. "And that brings us to our last victim...Mr. Franklin Dullard, a professor of law at the local university. He was known and praised for his intelligence and sharpness of mind. His works had been recognized by the crown. Quite impressive, truly."

I chewed the inside of my lip, peering around at all the articles and photographs. "But what ties them together?" I asked. "Apart from how they were killed.

Did they all happen to be walking down the same street where the killer was lying in wait? Or did they all perhaps have the same acquaintance, who ended up killing them?"

"It isn't entirely farfetched to believe that some of them might have known the same people," Mr. Keats said. "Though the last three victims were vastly different from one another, they all were quite well accepted in society, and likely had good connections with others. But then, what of the first victim? How does he tie in?"

Silence fell over us as we stared around at the photographs, hoping that inspiration would strike if only we paid closer attention.

There came the sound of a throat clearing, and I turned, surprised to find Mrs. Bell and Warrington hovering nearby. They must have come to help collect the dishes.

"Is there something you wish to say, Mrs. Bell?" I asked.

"Pardon me, I did not mean to overhear," Mrs. Bell said. "But with all this talk of death, I cannot help but think of another death that happened some years ago now... It was a terrible business, perhaps even more gruesome than these." She rubbed her arms with her hands, shivering. "Oh, good heavens...what was the victim's name? Victor Mayfield, I believe? No, Victor Norfolk. That was it."

Warrington turned to look at her. "Yes, I believe I recall the death you are speaking of. That case went unsolved as well, didn't it?"

Mr. Keats arched an eyebrow. "The name does not sound familiar to me," he said.

"Nor I," I echoed.

"You both would have been young," Mrs. Bell said, procuring a handkerchief from the pocket of her apron. "Perhaps no older than eighteen or nineteen years, madam. And you, Mr. Keats, not a great deal older."

He nodded. "I suppose that is true," he said, giving me a brief glance out of the corner of his eye.

"What about that man's death reminds you of these?" I asked.

"Well, as Mr. Warrington said, it was an unsolved case," Mrs. Bell said. "The man was horribly murdered...although not in the same way these victims have been."

"The body was left in a public street, brutally slashed and mangled," Warrington said.

"How could someone do that so clearly out in the open?" I asked.

"Somehow, the police developed the theory that it was a lover's quarrel," Warrington said. "The woman he was in love with may have been married, or seeing another man, and they assumed it might have been her jealous lover coming back for revenge."

"The word *liar* written across his chest in his own blood certainly seemed to help them infer that story..." Mrs. Bell said, stepping up to the table.

"But they never discovered who the lover was," Warrington said. "Or, who they assumed was the lover. Everyone in his life said he had never been married, and there wasn't anyone they were aware of that he had been seeing. If such a woman existed at all, she must have been a secret to those in his life."

"How bizarre..." Mr. Keats said.

"It was indeed," Warrington said, his gaze suddenly sharp as he peered down at the photograph of Commander Townsend. "For if I'm not mistaken, Mr. Norfolk was also in the navy. Not a commander, but I believe he held some sort of prestigious rank."

Mrs. Bell's brow furrowed. "Are you certain?" she asked. "I thought he was in the army."

"No," Warrington said. "I remember that part of his biography."

Then he picked up the picture of Mr. Frank Dullard, the professor.

His eyes widened. "And if I am not mistaken once again, he was attending a local university to pursue a law degree. I read that in the paper."

I chewed my lower lip in thought. "Those could be mere coincidences," I said.

But Mr. Keats was now perusing the information once again. "Is there any way we can find more information about this victim?" he asked. "You would not by any chance still have the paper with that article in it, would you?"

"No, I am afraid not..." Mrs. Bell said. "It was so long ago."

Mr. Keats's face hardened. "No matter. I know who would. Give me an hour and I shall be back with the information we need."

And without another word, he dashed out of the dining room.

I looked up at Mrs. Bell, who was staring after him. "Where do you suppose he's off to at this hour?"

"Scotland Yard, I would wager," Warrington said, tidying some of the notes that were now askew. "And I do not doubt he will find what he is looking for."

≈

AN AGONIZING HOUR and a half passed. I played with Daniel and watched his nanny put him to bed, and was just about to sit down in the parlor with some tea when Mr. Keats returned. Warrington let him into the parlor.

"I have the obituary," were the first words out of his mouth, his breathing ragged and heavy as if he had run the entire way. "The constable at the station didn't seem too keen on helping me, but once I managed to convince him I was who I said I was, he looked up the information I wanted and gave it to me."

"Excellent," I said. "Come in, I've had the servants move all the information to the wall in here. Warrington believes he might have a theory about the whole matter. However, I wish to hear whatever it was that you discovered, first."

Mr. Keats nodded, removing his top hat and tucking it beneath his arm. "You are not going to believe this..." he said, staring down at the papers clutched in his hand. "But I believe we may have stumbled upon the connection we were looking for."

I stared at him. "What sort of connection?"

He walked forward and set the papers down on the low table between the sofa and the chair nearest me.

"I give you Mr. Norfolk," he said, pointing to the photograph.

My heart caught in my throat. "Good heavens..." I breathed. "He looks...he could be his *twin* – "

Warrington moved to the wall as if I had asked him, pulling the pin from the wood and removing a photograph.

When he set it down beside the photo of Victor Norfolk, there was no mistaking it.

The first victim in the recent string of murders, the young Christopher Wedley...he looked very nearly identical to Victor Norfolk. Eerily similar. It was rather frightening.

"Are they related in some way?" I asked, peering up at Mr. Keats. "Did you see a similar surname in that obituary anywhere?"

"No," Mr. Keats said. "But that isn't where the similarities end." He glanced at my butler. "Mr. Warrington, you were indeed correct that he was in the royal navy. A lieutenant, in fact."

"Just a few ranks below Commander," Warrington said, his brow furrowing.

"Precisely," Mr. Keats said. "And you were correct once again. He was studying law at the university when he died. It seemed he had dreams to one day teach at the school himself, but knew he needed viable experience before he left the navy."

"That means he is connected to three of the recent victims," I said, counting them off on my fingers. "What of the fourth one? The accountant?"

"There's an answer for that, as well," Mr. Keats said, flipping through the papers he had brought back with him. "Look here. The various clubs he was a part of... both the White's Gentlemen's club, as well as the Athenaeum. Both prestigious, both very well known all throughout London, especially anyone who belongs to the Athenaeum."

"And those were the same clubs the third victim belonged to?" I asked.

Mr. Keats nodded.

This cannot be coincidence, can it?" I asked.

"These recent killings. They all tie back to that death some years ago."

"A death that many have likely forgotten almost entirely. I doubt many would even recognize the victim's name if it was mentioned," Mr. Keats said. "How could I have missed this? How did Scotland Yard?"

"I suppose these deaths were all removed enough from that first death to appear separate," I said. "The question now is, we know they are connected, but why? Is this the original killer coming back to kill again? Or is this the work of someone who is simply mimicking the horror of that first murder? Perhaps someone who found the whole thing fascinating?"

"That is the same question I kept asking myself, over and over, as I was walking back here," Mr. Keats said.

"It seems incredible," I said. "All these deaths relating back to that one man... Who was he? Why was he so important?"

"I have no idea," Mr. Keats said. "That is what we must aim to get to the bottom of. If we have learned anything, it is that this is indeed a planned event. Someone is either trying to recreate the original murder, or paying homage to it."

"But why?" I asked. "Only a disturbed mind would wish to do such a thing."

"It is indeed disturbing," Mr. Keats said. "And the

answer to your question, I believe, will lead us to the killer..."

I stared down at the papers spread out before us, seeing now a fifth face added to this already complex equation.

I knew there was something that tied them all together...though I never would have expected it to be another person.

"We must remain vigilant," Mr. Keats said. "This is likely going to become more difficult before it grows any easier. The killer has remained in the shadows for so long he may have grown complacent. If we are able to uncover the truth before he realizes we are hot on his trail, then we might, *might*, just be able to put a stop to this before anyone else is harmed."

I nodded. "That is what must be done, of course. We have no choice. We have discovered the truth, or at least a portion of it, and we must do what we can to ensure that whoever is committing these terrible crimes is brought to justice."

"Exactly," Mr. Keats said. "Now, the very best thing we can do next is..."

11

M r. Keats felt the best way we could progress forward with the case was if we were to divide ourselves.

Two different aspects of the case needed our attention. First, and perhaps foremost, was to uncover more information about Victor Norfolk's death. As it had been some years since he was killed, Mr. Keats insisted that he take that part of the case. His connections went a great deal deeper than my own, even with the use of my family name, and he knew that he would be able to find the information more quickly than I could.

As annoyed as I might have been, I knew very well that he was right, and due to our time constraints, it would be best for him to go and investigate that part of the case.

That left me with the responsibility to seek information about Christopher Wedley, the first victim in the Hyde Park murders.

"It would be best if you were to go around that part of town under a ruse," Mr. Keats explained. "Have a reason for being there. If you can get information out of the locals, then brilliant. But have a reason for going."

"Perhaps I might bring some paper advertisements to hang?" I suggested. "With the name of my business on them. I could ask the shopkeepers if I might hang them in the windows. That way I am still promoting my inquiry business, and yet at the same time, I am also there to ask questions."

I reflected bitterly on the fact that I was still reliant upon my father-in-law's generosity, so I spent the rest of the following morning copying my advertisements from the newspapers onto larger papers that could be read from shop windows.

As I stared down at the advertisements I'd been writing up, I worried about the whole affair. There was so much that could go wrong, so much that likely *would* go wrong. What would happen if we failed to capture the killer before he struck again? What if the string of murders became a never-ending cycle?

I tried to shake aside the thought. Surely we would catch the villain, eventually. We had already discovered perhaps the most important key to understanding the case. It was intimately tied to the death of the victim from so many years ago.

I collected the papers, and summoned Warrington to accompany me. Considering some of the places I might be going, it would have been unwise to proceed alone.

After checking the article about Christopher's death once again, Warrington and I found ourselves down past the southern part of Hyde Park, a few streets removed.

"The article said it happened in an alleyway to the south of the park," I murmured.

I peered down a narrower street of shops of varying kinds, staring back and forth between them. "We shall start with this first one on the corner," I said.

We entered shop after shop, asking first to hang the advertisements for my business in their windows. A few shopkeepers agreed, but most refused. When I did my best to casually ask about Christopher Wedley, no one wished to answer any questions. Two shopkeepers even chased me back out onto the street.

"They could simply tell me they did not wish to speak of it," I said, glaring back over my shoulder at one woman shaking her fist at me from the front steps. I adjusted my hat, blowing a stray hair out of my face. "Well, this certainly is not a success," I admitted.

"No, madam, it does not appear to be," Warrington said. "However, there are still more shops to try."

"I am beginning to doubt that anyone will actually agree to help us," I grumbled. "Still, I suppose it only takes one. Let us continue our efforts."

We walked down to the next door, which happened to be a small bakery. As we approached the front steps, the strong, warm smell of cinnamon washed over me, immediately putting my fears to rest. At the very least, we might be able to enjoy something sweet for all of our troubles.

The front of the bakery itself was quite small, with only two tables and a few mismatched chairs. The glass case at the back of the shop, which held cakes, muffins, scones, and pies, beckoned me with the fragrant aroma of vanilla and bright fruits.

"Good afternoon," said the woman behind the counter. She was a round, pudgy faced woman, with a kind smile and flecks of flour all over the front of her apron.

"Good afternoon," I said. "My name is Victoria Ward, and I was wondering if I might put up an advertisement in your window for my business?"

The woman's face furrowed slightly. "Oh..." she said. "Well, I am not one much for that sort of thing, as I fear it distracts customers from my own business."

I nodded. "I understand," I said. "Well then, perhaps you could help me with something else, instead. I am looking for information..."

I glanced over my shoulder at Warrington, who had remained near the door.

"Yes? What is it?" the baker asked.

"This may be rather uncomfortable to speak of," I said, repeating the same words I had used with the half dozen or so other people I had spoken with in the other shops. "But I wish to ask you about Christopher Wedley...the young man who was killed out here in the alleyway some time ago."

The baker's face went pale, and my heart sank. *I might as well turn and leave now.*

"That was such a terrible day for my family and me..." the woman said, her eyes welling with tears. "He was...he was such a good lad, and what happened to him was unspeakable..."

I looked over my shoulder once again at Warrington.

He nodded, and slipped outside. It had been our agreement that he keep watch while I spoke with the shopkeepers so we were not interrupted. Mr. Keats had suggested it, saying the killer might very well have spies around who would be keeping an eye on previous places they had been.

"You knew him?" I asked, pulling a clean handkerchief from its home tucked inside the sleeve of my dress. I passed it to the woman.

"Thank you..." she said, nodding her head. "And yes, we knew him. Not entirely too well, but well enough. Likely better than most of the others down the street here did."

"I do not wish to burden you," I said. "But would you be willing to tell me a little about him?"

She sniffed, dabbing at her eyes with the handkerchief. "Yes, I certainly can. Are you...connected with the police?"

"I am investigating his death," I said vaguely. "It is my hope that with some new information, the truth about what happened to him could be uncovered. Here, I shall buy a pastry from you, and perhaps a warm cup of tea, and we can sit down together and you can tell me what you know."

"Very well," the woman said. Before she turned to make her way back into the kitchen, she gave me a level look. "You said your name was Victoria Ward?"

My heart skipped for a moment. "Yes, I did," I said. I wondered if maybe she recognized me somehow, or perhaps there was someone else with that name.

She nodded. "I didn't wish to forget. My name is Margaret Green. My husband and I own this bakery together."

"It is truly one of the most charming in all of London," I said with a polite smile.

She smiled in return, and disappeared to fetch our tea.

A short while later, we sat down together at one of the small tables near the window. Each of us had a piping hot cup of tea – I insisted that she have one for herself – and a flaky, buttery tartlet sat before me. My mouth watered, but I refrained for a moment.

"There, now. This is very nice. Thank you, Mrs. Green," I said.

"It is my pleasure," she said. "Especially if you can help us get to the bottom of that poor boy's death…"

"What can you tell me about him?" I asked. "Very little information was obtained about him at the time of his death. Do you happen to know anything of his past? Or perhaps anything of his relationships?"

"We did not know a great deal ourselves," Mrs. Green said, frowning into her teacup. "He was around twenty-five years of age when we met him, I think. Handsome as well, incredibly so. Many of the young girls hereabouts, including my own daughters, were quite smitten with him." Her ghost of a smile faded quickly. "When he started coming around here, he had no place to live, and was simply trying to find someone to hire him. It seemed he came from working in the theater. He had been an actor and entertainer, most likely due to his good looks and pleasant singing voice. But after a time, he was no longer needed at the theatre and was thrown out."

"And he had no family? No friends to take him in?" I asked.

She shook her head. "His parents died when he was younger, just before he joined the theater. He had no siblings, and his grandparents moved away some ten years ago. And all of his friends were in the theater group. When it came down to it, it seemed their loyalties lay with the theater as opposed to one another."

"How unfortunate for him," I said.

"Indeed," Mrs. Green said with a heavy sigh. "When he arrived here, he had been all over the city looking for work. He knew he was a handsome young man, so he realized that he could very well find something of value in the wealthier parts of the city. The jobs he chose never lasted long, though. Some were simple, such as an artist wishing to use his likeness for a painting, which they would pay him quite poorly for. There were others, as well. Some ladies would hire him as extra help to wait on guests at parties or to entertain the guests. They liked his pretty face, but would never keep him around long."

"So what was it that led to his death?" I asked.

My question was interrupted by the sound of a yelp outside the bakery, causing both of us to jump.

"What was that?" Mrs. Green asked in a terrified whisper.

Another scream, male, echoed from outside.

Immediately, my thoughts leaped to Warrington, who had been waiting outside.

I launched myself from the chair and rushed to the door, not wasting a second.

Hurrying outside, I nearly fell down the stairs

when I saw Warrington sprawled out on the street, clutching at his chest.

I came to a halt beside him, kneeling down. "Warrington, what happened?" I cried.

Panting, he stared up at me, moving his hand which he held clutched over his heart. Blood leaked from between his fingers.

12

"Mrs. Sedgewick?"

My eyes shot open, and I jumped from my seat. "Yes? What is it?" I asked.

It was the middle of the night. I had taken refuge in the drawing room on the second floor, the room nearest Warrington's private quarters. I had fallen asleep in an armchair, the last of the embers of the fire still glowing in the hearth of the fireplace beside me.

Doctor Higgins reached out to help steady me. "Easy now, Mrs. Sedgwick. I did not mean to startle you."

I blinked the sleep from my eyes, attempting to gather myself once more. "It's quite all right. How is he?"

Doctor Higgins pushed his spectacles up the bridge

of his nose, sighing heavily. "He seems to be stable. The wound was not deep, but it was quite long. I imagine the culprit managed to drag the blade across his chest as opposed to burying it in any further, which very well may have saved his life."

"So he is going to survive, then?" I asked.

Doctor Higgins nodded. "As far as I can see, yes. I expect he is going to survive. He is required, however, to stay on bed rest, and I have instructed Mr. Tulson and Mrs. Bell how to change the bandages over his chest. I shall remain here for another hour or so in case he takes a turn for the worse, but I thought you would wish to know as soon as possible how he fares."

"Yes, of course," I said, smoothing out my skirts. "Might I go in and visit him?"

"I can see no reason why not," the doctor said. "But do not stay long enough to tire him."

I nodded, and hurried out of the drawing room and down the corridor.

I was not prepared for what I saw when I stepped through the doorway into the butler's room.

Warrington lay in his bed, pillows propped around him, his arms stretched out over the blankets that were drawn up to his waist. His head was back against the pillows, and his face was as pale as the sheets that were spread out beneath him.

The nightshirt he wore was open at the chest, and a

broad white bandage was fixed to the place where the wound was, just over his heart.

I hovered in the doorway. It was the first time since I'd known Warrington that he looked old. In all the time he had been with my family, I had never thought of him as weak or tired. Yet there he was, lying prostrate on the bed, looking as helpless as an infant.

As if sensing my presence, Warrington lifted his head slightly, his eyes opening slowly. "Ah, madam," he said in a croaky, weak voice. "How kind of you to come..."

I summoned my courage to enter the room. "You must save your strength, Warrington," I said, going to the side of his bed.

He gave me a weak smile. "I apologize that I cannot get out of bed," he said. "Doctor Higgins has forbidden me from getting back on my feet for the next three days."

"I know," I said. "And you must not apologize. It is completely fine. I wish you to rest." My calm façade wavered for a moment then. "I am so sorry this happened, Warrington..." I said, my eyes stinging with tears. "I do not even know what to say, what to think –"

The butler looked embarrassed by my display of emotion. "There is nothing for you to apologize for, madam," he assured me quickly. "No one could have predicted this would happen."

"We are very fortunate the police reached you

when they did," I said. "I was terrified that the wound was too severe. The amount of blood that you left behind on the street – "

Those moments after he had been attacked were nothing more than a blur in my mind. Fear had taken hold of my thoughts, and I had been able to do little, apart from attempting to slow Warrington's bleeding by applying pressure to the wound with my kerchief. Bystanders had gone to fetch help.

Somehow, we had got Warrington back to the house, where Doctor Higgins was sent for. He advised that it would be best not to move Warrington to the hospital or anywhere else, as long as there were sufficient hands to care for him here at the house.

"What happened?" I asked Warrington now. "When I was inside the bakery, how were you attacked?"

Warrington let out a dry, heaving cough.

I waited nervously for him to finish.

His breathing came in wheezes as he wiped the back of his hand over his mouth. I noticed that his hands were shaking.

"I was keeping watch, just as we agreed," he said. "It was very quiet. Not a soul in sight. And in the middle of the afternoon, the most I had expected to see were women finishing errands for their families, or perhaps cooks collecting their goods for the evening..."

He licked his lips, which seemed cracked and swollen.

"Here, let me get you a little water," I said, turning to the white ceramic pitcher that Mrs. Bell must have brought in to leave on the side table. I poured a tall glass and brought it over to him.

I helped lift his head and let him take a few, feeble sips.

"Thank you," he said, smacking his lips.

I set down the glass.

"We may discuss this later, if you prefer," I said. "You truly should rest. It is late, and – "

"No," Warrington said, giving a small shake of his head. "I should tell you everything while it is fresh in my memory. I think it important to the case."

"What do you mean? What did you see?" I asked.

"The man who attacked me," he said. "He came from behind me, from between the shops. He was a small man, extremely short, and he had only one eye."

I stared down at him. "One eye? Are you certain about that?" A one-eyed attacker sounded a little too much like a villain from a novel.

Nonetheless, Warrington nodded. "Most of his face was covered when he launched himself at me, but his hood fell backward when I attempted to fight back. He hadn't expected that, clearly. There was something long and sharp in his hand, almost like a needle. I knocked it away before he was able to stick me with it, which I think was his intention. He managed to get the knife in me before I realized what was happening. Clearly, he was angry that I had spotted him."

"Why does the one eye sound familiar..." I wondered.

"Because another one-eyed man was in the report of the first death," said Warrington. "He had been lurking near the body, but vanished before anyone was able to speak with him."

"So all of these deaths do tie together," I said.

"I believe they do," Warrington said. "I am not sure what to make of it all...other than I wonder if I was meant to be the next victim."

I stared down at him. "You...a victim?"

Warrington nodded. "I wonder in what way I had a connection to the original death. I must have, somehow."

"Well, you are safe now," I said. "We will take care of you, and Doctor Higgins said you are going to get well again. You simply need to rest."

"I know," he said. "You must not worry about me, madam. You must focus on your own safety. If the killer is beginning to realize that you are investigating, then you may be in danger yourself. Take care, won't you?"

"Of course, Warrington," I said. "I promise I shall."

13

...*And now he is resting at home, with doctor's orders to remain in bed and instructions left for my staff to change his bandages every few hours. To say this has been a trying time would be a drastic under-statement.*

I looked up from the letter I was in the process of writing, and stared out the window at the warm sunshine streaming inside.

It was just before sunset. After realizing Warrington was safe, I had spent a few hours attempting to get some sleep. It was a futile effort, however. The dreams that haunted me prevented me from any sort of real rest, so instead I fixed my attention on Daniel and on checking in on Warrington while he slept. And sleep he did. After my first visit in the middle of the night, he fell into a deep, hard sleep.

I stood in the butler's doorway with Daniel in my arms for long stretches of time, staring in at him.

"He'll be all right," I assured my small son, though I knew little Daniel had no earthly idea what was happening around him, why everyone was so hushed and sad. "Don't you worry, little one. Everyone in this house is going to be just fine."

But the longer my butler slept, the more fearful I became.

"It is good for him to rest," Mrs. Bell said mid-morning as she changed his bandages. I tried my best not to look at the amount of blood that had seeped into the old, dirty wrappings. "The more he rests, the faster he will be able to heal."

Even still, I worried that he would sleep forever and be unable to wake.

After giving the baby his afternoon feeding, I tucked him into his bassinet beside me in the study, and sat down to write Mr. Keats a letter about the latest goings on.

I twirled my pen in the air for a moment or two, trying to figure out how to tell him what my next plan was.

I hope the information I uncovered concerning Christo-pher Wedley will be of use to you. Mrs. Green was incred-

ibly kind, and I am certain if you have any further questions, she will be able to help you.

As for the one-eyed man, I believe he is the key to finding the killer, if he isn't the killer himself. From the way I see it, Warrington may very well be the first person to have seen him and survived to give a full description. If he was attempting to capture Warrington, intending for him to be the next victim, then we are quite fortunate Warrington was able to fight off the attack.

I looked up, troubled. "We are fortunate, indeed..."

I have a plan, Mr. Keats. A plan you will very likely frown upon, but I cannot sit back any longer, knowing that this madman attempted to kidnap my butler for his dark purposes. The matter has become quite personal. I am going to help you to get to the bottom of this, and I hope that together, we can put an end to these mysterious killings.

By the time you read this letter, my plan will likely already be put into action. I do hope you will forgive my haste, and I hope even more than this that my investigations will prove fruitful. I shall write to you as soon as I have completed them.

I signed the letter and set it aside to dry, my name glistening in black ink across the bottom of the paper.

∼

I WAS nervous all throughout dinner that evening. Eliza had brought Daniel in to eat with me, mostly as a means of keeping him occupied. Mr. Tulson had temporarily taken over Warrington's duties, without complaint and with great care.

"We want everything to be running smoothly for him when he recovers," Mr. Tulson said with a smile.

I hardly touched my first course, a pumpkin soup, and found my appetite was very nearly absent when Mrs. Bell brought up a roasted duck from Corbyn down in the kitchen. It was one of my favorite meals, but I also recalled Warrington once saying it was one of his favorites.

"I am sorry, Mrs. Bell," I said. "I simply cannot stop thinking about Warrington. It is so distressing, what happened to him."

"I understand entirely," she said, setting down my plate before me. "But you must eat. If not for yourself, then for the little master. Mr. Warrington would also be very unhappy to know that you had refused food on his account."

I sighed, and did my best to take at least a few small bites.

"Was he doing all right?" Eliza asked the house-keeper in a low voice. "I have not been in to see him since last night."

"His breathing seems to be steadier," Mrs. Bell said. "But he still has a long way to go. The next few days will be crucial to ensure that he begins to heal. Doctor Higgins will be over again in the morning to check on his progress, and to bring something for the pain, if he needs it."

I interrupted their conversation. "I believe I shall go out this evening," I announced.

Mrs. Bell looked startled. "Where could you possibly have to go tonight, madam?" she asked. "Surely it could wait until daylight."

I shook my head. "It is something for the case," I said. "I promised Mr. Keats I would look into it, and as I lost so much time today, I think I might go and see what I can do before it's too late."

Mrs. Bell frowned in concern. "I wish you would reconsider," she said. "Without Mr. Warrington to go with you, especially in the dark..."

"I shall be careful," I said. "And I shouldn't be gone more than an hour. It is not very far."

"Are you going to see that Mrs. Green again?" Mrs. Bell asked, her eyes darting down to my barely touched plate.

"I very well might do that at a later time," I said. "But no, this is something much closer to home. And night is the best time for me to go and look."

∽

AT A QUARTER PAST TEN, Mr. Tulson helped me into my traveling cloak.

"Are you certain you must go out, madam?" he asked hesitantly.

"Yes," I said. "I must get to the bottom of this, for Warrington's sake. But do not worry. I shall not linger any longer than I must. In the meantime, take care of everyone until I return."

"Yes, of course," Mr. Tulson said, and he opened the door for me.

The night air rushed in over the threshold, sending my cloak fluttering out behind me. The wind rattled through the bushes and the branches of the low, small trees in front gardens up and down the street. My heart beat rapidly as I stepped down onto the sidewalk that I had tread so many times before. It now felt like foreign ground to me.

The street itself was very nearly silent. Windows glowed bright and warm as I hurried from one pool of light to the next, cast by the street lamps alongside the cobblestone road. They invited me, encouraged me to turn around and return home.

But the desire for answers propelled me onward.

I need to know. If the murderer is attempting to make another kill, then I need to see for myself.

A drunken man stumbled along on the other side of the street, singing a sea shanty as he nearly walked into a stone planter in front of a neighboring home. I kept my distance and kept my head low. It was best if he did not spot me. I needed no unpleasant encounters interrupting my mission.

Soon, I made it to the end of the street, and turned to see the dark, shadowed green that was Hyde Park.

I looked up and down the street, though I knew full well that there would likely be few carriages at this hour, and then I hurried across to the open expanse of grass and trees.

It looked much more forbidding at night. The shadows the trees cast seemed like spindly arms and pointed claws, while the swaying branches rattled and snapped against one another as the wind passed through them, making my heart pound as I walked beneath them.

I pulled my cloak more tightly around my shoulders, my nerves leaping with every noise I heard.

I told myself that I must keep calm and find what I was looking for. Only then could I return home.

As I walked, the courage I had so easily felt at home dwindled. Fear sapped me of my strength, and I questioned my purpose here. What was the likelihood, after all, that I would just randomly happen upon the killer or some evidence of him?

Nevertheless, I pushed forward, eager to do what I came for so I could go home and be with my infant son again. Holding baby Daniel seemed far more preferable in that moment than wandering through Hyde Park at night.

I came to the place where I had been just a few days before, when the body of Mr. Dullard had been found.

I was entirely out in the open, so I ducked behind a tree, clinging to the shadows.

The killer tends to leave bodies in this park, but not in any one particular place. What are the chances he would hide the body here once again?

Unfortunately for me, the park was a large area, and it would take me hours to search the whole of it.

A flash of light up ahead caught my attention, and I hid myself fully in the shadow of the tree. My heart thundering in my ears, I chanced a look, peering out from behind the trunk.

I recognized the hat of a constable near the clearing where Mr. Dullard's body had been found. It was difficult to make out what exactly he was doing, but from the sweeping motion of the light from the lantern in his hand, it was clear he was checking the area.

I watched him as he moved back and forth several times, keeping close to the same area.

Either he is guarding that spot, or he is searching for something...

It was difficult to tell which, as I couldn't see any other constables about.

Perhaps Mr. Keats managed to convince the authorities they did not have the real killer in custody after all. If that is so, then it's likely they are watching the park, in case the murderer decides to strike again.

I chewed on the inside of my lip. If they were here, then was there really any need for me to be?

Likely not.

I breathed a small sigh of relief. Perhaps it would be just as well for me to –

I swatted at something on the back of my neck, feeling a prick, like the bite of an insect.

I pulled my hand away and tried to examine what I'd managed to squash, but found only a bead of blood there.

As I stared, the air around me began to waver, and the bead of blood began to spin in circles. My head grew heavy, as did my eyelids.

What...what happened?

All at once, I felt my body going limp, and I toppled over backward.

Something, or someone, caught me. A silhouette peered down at me, the dim light from the lampposts beyond shielding the person's face from my view.

I opened my mouth to speak, to question, but my numb tongue could not form any words.

Sleep pressed in on me from all sides, an exhaustion that I had never known before.

Soon, there was nothing I could do apart from giving in, allowing the darkness to overtake me.

14

The next time I opened my eyes, I had to squint against the brightness that was in such great contrast to the darkness I had been surrounded in.

Except...I thought I had just closed my eyes. I thought I was still in Hyde Park, looking for evidence of the killer.

It took a moment for me to realize the velvety fabric tucked up against my cheek smelled of lilac and rosemary. It was soothing, warm, inviting.

The only sound in the room was the soft *tick, tock, tick, tock* of a clock. It sounded nothing like the one I usually kept in my bedroom. *Did Warrington change the clock? Did Mrs. Bell buy a new one?*

My mind began to work slowly, to process my surroundings.

I have never owned anything that smells quite like this...and while it feels wonderful to rest upon, it cannot be in my bedroom. Can it?

I tried to force my eyelids open, but they resisted.

It would be so much easier to simply...go back to sleep...

But a sudden burst of fear shot through me, clearing my mind.

Who had the silhouette in the park belonged to? What had happened?

I opened my eyes again and blinked at the sudden, bright light. My vision was blurred as I stared around, but my mind became clearer, filled with panic, as I realized that the room in which I found myself was entirely new to me.

I had never been here in my life.

I found myself lying on a bed covered in a bright pink coverlet of crushed velvet. Stacked with frilly pillows and a soft blanket stretched across the foot of the bed, beneath my feet, it was much larger than my own bed at home, and twice as luxurious.

The room itself was quite sizable, with polished furnishings, a large bay window, and ancient, antique pieces that looked as if they must have each cost a small fortune. They included a rug, a vase, a series of blazing lamps, and a golden statue of a woman pouring water from a jug.

I sat up, my heart thundering in my chest.

Where in the world am I?

I reached around to the back of my neck, and felt the skin where I'd been pricked. My hand came away clean, but the spot was rather tender.

Did someone drug me?

Goosebumps crept up my arms as I looked around.

The ticking from the clock on the wall made me that much more uneasy, as it was the only sound I heard.

If someone brought me here, then I am obviously not alone...

There was only one way to find out what was happening.

I crossed to the door and pressed an ear against it, waiting to see if I heard anything out in the corridor.

When nothing could be clearly heard on the other side, I chanced a peek by grabbing the handle and pulling it open.

Some relief washed over me. *I half expected it to be locked...*

I stared through a narrow gap into the hall beyond, surprised at how suddenly familiar it felt. The blue of the walls tugged at something in my mind, as if I were seeing it through the eyes of a child.

I looked up and down the corridor, seeing no one, and no movement.

In the distance, however, music played as if some sort of party was happening.

I hurried down the hall, doing my best to keep my

footsteps light and silent. I had no earthly idea where I was headed, but knew that as soon as I found a staircase, I was that much closer to being able to leave.

The stillness of the massive home was unsettling. I passed room after room, each with their doors ajar, and no one inside. Not a soul seemed to be here, yet every lamp in the place was aglow.

It must be very nearly midnight by now. What was happening here?

I came around a corner and found myself in a grand foyer, three stories from the bottom. I peered over a polished walnut banister down to the black and white tile floor, and saw that tucked away beneath a marble portico was the front door.

This place seems so familiar to me... Why? What is it about this house that has me so curious?

The music grew louder, increasing in volume. It sounded as if a full orchestra was playing somewhere.

I shook my head. It was as though my head wanted to turn inside out. This was all so utterly bizarre.

It didn't matter. I needed to escape. I needed to return home, return to Daniel.

I started down the stairs, careful not to trip in my haste, yet also doing my best to keep my footsteps soft. If my captor was anywhere about, I did not wish to be discovered.

Nearly out of breath, I reached the bottom landing, my feet striking the tiled floor.

Almost out!

I hurried toward the front entrance, but as I did so, I passed two large glass doors that had been thrown open, yellow light pouring from inside and out into the hall –

I stopped in my tracks.

I have been here before...

The memory was faint. Broken. Somewhere far in the back of my mind, I recalled being in a place very similar to this, experiencing a great crowd of people, music, elegant decorations for the Christmas season, and lavish arrays of food.

But why am I here of all places?

I took a hesitant step forward. There was not a soul inside, but the ballroom just beyond the door was exactly as I remembered it.

The windows along the eastern wall stretched from floor to ceiling, draped in heavy red velvet curtains. The floor itself, made of polished wood with an inlaid design of roses in the center of the room, reflected the light of the chandeliers overhead, each of which was lit and glowing brightly.

"I was wondering when you would make an appearance..." came a sultry voice, almost like a purr. "It took you longer to wake than I expected."

My heart nearly leapt from my chest as I wheeled around.

A woman sat in a golden, high backed chair along the wall, its partner beside her sitting empty.

She was beautiful, with hair the color of a raven's wings, so deeply dark it was nearly blue. Her skin was flawless over her high cheekbones, and she had full red lips, and thick eyelashes. Her eyes were a piercing shade of green, like cut emeralds that glistened in the light. A playful smile tugged at her lips, and she sat casually against the back of her chair as if without a care in the world.

Her dress was rather scandalously cut, and made of a deep scarlet silk. Her gloves, the same color, were pulled up to her elbows.

A gramophone was set up beside her, playing the music I'd been hearing from upstairs. It was astounding that such a small machine could make such a large sound in the cavernous ballroom.

"It is a pleasure to meet you," the woman said in the same sultry voice. "Or, at least, I thought it would be. You are not the sort of person I would have expected to figure out my secret."

I stared at her. Could this be the killer? Somehow, I had never considered the idea that the murderer might be a woman. The crimes had required an element of strength, so I had assumed the culprit was male. Then too, Warrington had described his attacker as a man...

The mysterious woman suddenly looked to her

right and snapped her fingers. "Bartholomew. Fetch our guest a seat, won't you?"

I turned to see who she was speaking to, and I barely contained a gasp.

A man with one eye smiled at her, bowing his awkward, short body very nearly in half. His broad chin and sunken cheeks made me think he was a gargoyle come to life. "Yes, Mistress. Right away, Mistress."

He turned and scurried off, a slight limp to his left side.

So Warrington's description of him was an accurate one...

The woman's glittering gaze returned to me. "What is your name?" she asked, crossing her long legs at the knee. "I should like to know you better."

The words were lost on me as I continued staring at her. "You are the murderer?"

The woman rolled her eyes toward the ceiling. "Yes, I thought that much was obvious when I had my servant snatch you out of the park. I could not have you creeping around the next potential spot for my victim, now, could I?"

I frowned. "Who are you?" I asked.

She smiled, an expression more malicious than kind. "My name is not terribly important. Truly. It would only complicate matters."

I shrugged. "It is not as if I will be telling anyone. I

don't imagine you intend to allow me to walk out of here, do you?"

"Of course I could never do that," she agreed, leaning back in her seat. "I am not a fool or I would have been caught long before this, do you not think? To let you go after you've seen my face would be impossible. Still, I thought it best to bring you here because it has been such a long time since I have had a friend to talk to. I thought you might provide me with some pleasant company before I kill you."

I was careful to keep my face expressionless, although the frankness with which she spoke sent chills down my spine. If she really was the one responsible for all the horrific deaths that had happened over the past weeks, it was clear she had no remorse for her deeds. It was equally clear that she possessed the ability to carry out her threat against me. Her previous actions had proven that.

Part of me wondered if I might buy time by pleading for my life. I had an infant son, after all, who would be left an orphan with my death. Perhaps informing her of that would soften her heart.

But she did not strike me as the sort of woman who would listen to pleading.

No. If I was going to escape this place, I needed to remain as calm as I could, and try and figure out a way to best her, to catch her off guard. Perhaps a distraction, or –

"You are trying to think of a way out," the woman observed with a smirk. "I can see it in your eyes. I like that about you, the way you do not give up easily. Very well, how about we exchange initials, yes? I shall give you mine, if you give me yours first."

Initials. That was strange, wasn't it? Either she cared that little for me and my life, or she was just playing games.

Or perhaps she was testing me. How could I be certain she did not already know more about me than she was letting on?

"Very well..." I said, straightening. "You may call me V."

"V," the woman said, raising her eyebrows in curiosity. "Oh, how interesting. Pleased to make your acquaintance, V. You may call me Z."

Z. Is she lying? Or is that truly the first letter of her name?

Regardless, it was more than I knew even a few moments before.

"Here we are, Mistress," said the gargoyle man, returning with a rickety, wooden stool.

"Very good. Set it down there for her," Z said, grinning at me. "I should like her to keep me company."

Bartholomew set the stool down before me, his large single eye staring at me beadily.

I looked away, taking a seat on the stool.

"I should like to ask you some questions," Z said,

leaning forward with her chin resting in the palm of her hand. "If you answer them truthfully, I will allow you a few questions of your own. I can see you are full of them, after all."

I swallowed. What choice did I have? Anyway, it was to my advantage to buy myself time in order to figure out how I was going to escape.

I nodded in acceptance of her suggestion.

She giggled, a strange sound coming from a grown woman. "Excellent. My first question, then, is how you discovered it was me behind the murders. I wish to know where I went wrong so it does not happen again in the future."

So she did intend to kill again. In that case, whatever I did next would be to save, not only myself, but some future victim. Perhaps more than one. There was no telling how many more people she intended to harm. Knowing that, I realized I must swallow my fears and keep my wits about me. I couldn't afford to panic.

"To be quite honest, Z, I did not know it was you," I said. "I thought it was your servant, Bartholomew."

Z gasped, turning her amused expression over to her servant. "Did you hear that, Barty? She thought it was *you*."

The man laughed along with her, though it sounded a great deal more like wheezing than laughter.

"I can understand how you might think that, especially as he was the one fetching my victims, as well as bringing their corpses to the park, setting them up just so for me. But how did you come to know anything about him?" she asked.

Once again, I was put into a situation where I was unsure what to tell her. Should I tell her the truth about Warrington? Or would that further put him, and the rest of my household, at risk? I did not want her sending her servant to my home, possibly to silence Warrington and everyone else he might have already spoken to.

But the glint in her eyes reminded me of a serpent, and I had the sudden sense that if I lied, she would know it. Whereas if I was honest, she might very well answer my questions truthfully as well. It was a gamble I would have to take.

"He attacked my butler," I said. "Just yesterday, in fact."

Z's eyes widened. "Your butler?" she asked. "Well, isn't it such a small world?"

"You did not know?" I asked.

She grinned. "Perhaps I did, perhaps I didn't..."

An uncomfortable prickle ran down my spine. *She's toying with me.*

She tossed her long, thick curls over her shoulder. "I imagine you would like to know why I targeted him, wouldn't you?" she asked.

"I already know the answer to why you attacked my

servant," I said. "At least, I know part of it. It relates in some way to Victor Norfolk who was murdered, and put on display out in a public street a few years ago."

There was a dangerous flash in Z's eyes, and a toothy smile spread across her lovely face. She twirled a curl around the tip of her finger. "So you truly did discover it..." she said. "The connection between the recent murders and that one."

Was she proud? Or angry? It was difficult to know from the grin alone.

"I should like to tell you a story, Miss V, seeing as you have figured out my little secret," she said. Then she gasped. "No. I shall not tell you. Why don't you try and see if you can figure out why it was that I killed Victor all those years ago. Go on, do not be shy."

My thoughts raced as I attempted to discern her reason for asking. Was she testing me once again? Or was this nothing more than a ploy, an amusing way for her to pass the time?

"I..." I said. There were so many possibilities. "I take it that Mr. Norfolk wronged you in some way?"

"Wronged me would be a grand understatement," Z said. "He and I were in love once. For three blissful months, we were nearly inseparable. He was in the navy, so quite busy, but whenever we could be together, we were. He had grand ambitions for his life, and he promised time and again that I would be right there alongside him as he accomplished his goals. And I believed him. I believed every word that came out of his mouth…"

Her right hand balled into a fist, her knuckles turning white. Her smile grew, stretching across her face in a wicked sneer.

"My love for him grew and grew, but he began to withdraw," she said. "I asked him why, but he always avoided the answer. I asked if he had found some other woman, and he assured me he had not. I asked if the navy was keeping him busy, and he told me that was only part of it. Finally, he admitted that I was *too* much in love with him, that he feared I was developing an obsession that was not healthy for my mind. He was unnerved by my jealousy."

She slammed her fist onto the arm of the chair, the sound reverberating throughout the room.

"I told him that I loved him. Was that not what he wanted? I worshipped the ground he walked upon. I adored him with everything I had in me. I loved him more than life itself!"

Her lips split as she stared up at the ceiling, her voice growing in volume, and she laughed, a terrible sound.

"And do you know what he did, V? Do you know what he did to me?" she asked, her glassy gaze returning to me.

I was not brave enough to answer.

"He said he didn't wish to be with me anymore,"

she said. "He called off our engagement, told me that he never wished to see me again. I did not understand. I thought he would *value* my affection, my life, my all..."

The flash in her eyes returned.

"So I killed him," she said. "If I couldn't have him, then no one would. And I arranged his corpse in a public place, where he would be viewed by all, just as I imagined my humiliating rejection had been visible to many."

"How did the police fail to catch you?" I asked. "If you were engaged to marry this man – "

"They did not know," she said. "Despite my suspicions, it ultimately seems that he kept our love a secret from everyone in his life. When things became too serious, he became frightened and fled. But I could not forget him. Under the circumstances, what else was I to do?"

Let him go? Move on with your life?

"But my love for Victor still burns strong," she went on. "Once I moved past my grief, I realized there must be someone out there like him, someone who I could love the way I loved him. So I began my search, looking for the perfect man to replace Victor in my life."

The revelation passed over me, stilling me. "All these men that died...they were similar to Victor in some way."

"Now you understand," Z said, returning to her calm self, leaning back in her chair.

I continued to work it out aloud. "Mr. Dullard was a professor at a university, and Victor wished to teach there one day."

She nodded. "Very good."

"And Mr. Locke had all the same connections, and very likely knew Victor at one point or another," I said.

"Yes, and Commander Townsend was in the navy, and Christopher looked almost exactly like my Victor..." she said with a contented sigh, staring off into the distance rather dreamily.

Then her neck snapped upward, and the steely look in her eyes sent chills racing down my spine, making me want to run for the door.

"But none of them would love me. I lured them here, told them of what I could offer, but none of them would listen... For some reason, they did not trust me. They thought me mad."

"So you killed them, just like you did Victor," I said.

"Precisely," she said. "It is no matter, of course. I will find my suitable replacement for Victor, sooner or later. In the meantime, I have accumulated quite a reputation in the city, it seems." She chuckled. "Not to mention all the wealth and spoils I have. This house, for instance, belonged to my dear Mr. Locke."

I stared around. Mr. Locke? Why did this place seem so familiar to me, then?

Then it hit me. Locke was a name I had heard before, but when I was much younger.

His parents had known my parents. I had come to this house when I was very young for a Christmas ball.

"But why my butler?" I asked, pulling myself from my reverie. "Exactly what tied him to your Victor?"

"It was actually a matter of chance," she said. "I passed by your butler out in the street. I noticed he bore a striking resemblance to an older Victor, so I acted on sudden impulse and immediately sent Bartholomew to fetch him. But Barty was clumsy. He is used to careful planning and isolated locations, you see, and we had never tried anything this open and bold. He panicked and failed in his mission."

"Yes, my servant would not have been easily snatched off the street," I said. "He has his old military training."

She nodded. "No matter about him. I do apologize, Miss V, that your curiosity brought you into this situation. You are a slightly clever woman, and I could truly use an intelligent companion to talk with. Barty, as you see, is quite dull-witted. But I can see from the judgment in your eyes that you would never allow me to get away with murder. You do not wish for me to be happy. You simply wish to escape here with your life –"

There came a sudden banging sound from the foyer, making both of us jump.

"Barty, what was – "

She did not have time to finish her words. There was a rush of motion from the doors leading into the ballroom, and half a dozen men dressed in police uniforms and hats poured inside.

Trailing in behind them was Mr. Keats, his ever present top hat fixed atop his head.

His eyes fell on me, and he stopped in his tracks.

"Miss Victoria?" he asked, obviously startled. "What are you doing here?"

"It seems we came to the same conclusion, Mr. Keats, though I arrived a little sooner than you did," I said, getting to my feet, my knees weak with relief. "I present to you our killer."

15

"More tea, madam?"

"Yes, that would be lovely, thank you."

It was early the next morning. I was back at home, safe and sound, happily within the four walls of my own space. I had not been able to sleep, nor did I think I would for some time...at least until the excitement – or terror – of the night's events had worn off sufficiently.

"And you, sir?" asked Mrs. Bell, standing beside the trolley she had brought with her into the parlor, the room where I had remained ever since arriving home.

"I could never say no to your tea, Mrs. Bell," Mr. Keats said from his spot in the chair beside the fireplace.

She smiled as she turned back to the teapot. "I

cannot thank you enough, sir, for bringing our mistress home to us all."

"It was my pleasure," Mr. Keats said, turning his clear grey eyes onto me.

Mrs. Bell set down the tea before us, making mine just the way I liked it.

She bowed herself from the room, and closed the door behind her.

The *tick, tock* of the clock on the wall, a sound that was typically soothing, now set me slightly on edge. I turned my attention to Mr. Keats.

"I'm quite amazed that you were able to discern the truth just in time to save me," I said. "I was in such awe of my captor. I knew I had to find a way out of her house, but I had not yet formed any plan, except to delay my fate. I do not know what I would have done if you hadn't come."

"To be honest, Miss Victoria, I have to attribute my discovering the identity of the killer to you," he said. "I received your note just before nine o'clock last night, and with some digging, as well as help from the metropolitan police, I was able to narrow down who that one-eyed man was associated with. Fortunately, his appearance as well as a prior record of violence made him distinctive. As soon as I knew who employed him, there was no reason to hesitate in arresting the woman called Zara, your 'Miss Z'. There was no doubt that she would likely strike again, and what was to stop her from doing so last night?"

I smiled at him. "I suspect you would have arrived at the truth eventually without my help."

"But perhaps not before it was too late for someone," Mr. Keats said.

I picked up my teacup and sipped it. "So what happens next?" I asked. "What will happen to her?"

"Well, she will be tried before a court of law," Mr. Keats said. "I assume she will plead guilty, though even if she does not, there are now witnesses who have heard it straight from her own mouth...including you," he said with a pointed look at me. "I am sorry to say that you may be called upon to give testimony of what happened last night."

"I would be happy to give it," I said. "Anything to ensure that her actions will never be repeated."

"Good," Mr. Keats said. "I am pleased to hear it."

He pulled a gold watch on a chain from the pocket of his waistcoat and glanced at it.

"Are you in some hurry?" I asked.

"Only a little," he said. "I have another case I must get back to, and of course there is still the matter involving your late husband's death. I still intend to look further into that..."

He rose from his seat, his tea untouched.

"For now, I should allow you to rest," he said. "I have no doubt these past few days have been trying.

No one should ever have to experience what you did last night."

I nodded. "Thank you again, Mr. Keats," I said. "I feel much safer knowing that dreadful woman and her servant have both been arrested."

"Indeed," he said, spinning his top hat between his fingers. He cleared his throat. "Well then, I shall bid you farewell, Miss Victoria. I shall be in touch."

"Have a good day, Mr. Keats," I said.

He bowed his head, and turned to leave the room.

I continued to sip my tea after he had gone, thinking over the events of the previous several hours.

When Mr. Keats had entered that ballroom where I was held captive, I had never been so relieved in my life. As soon as I saw him, I knew that I was safe, that the terrible woman and her servant would never be able to harm me.

That feeling surprised me, given the fact that I had once disliked the private inquiry agent. After Duncan's death, I had resented the detective's intrusion into my home. He had certainly proven himself capable, however, and had gone above and beyond since then, in order to help me.

Perhaps Mr. Keats was more valuable than I had realized before.

Rising from my seat, I stifled a yawn. My limbs were heavy and aches covered my body. I decided it was time to tuck myself in for a nice, long nap.

I stepped out into the hall, wandering down toward the staircase in the foyer.

"Ah, madam, Mr. Keats just left," Mrs. Bell said from the middle of the stairs as she descended. "I thought it was kind of him to personally return you home."

"Indeed it was," I said.

Mrs. Bell smiled. "Oh, and I should tell you. I just looked in on Mr. Warrington, and his wound looks a great deal better this morning. He has already begun to rattle off tasks for Mr. Tulson to see to, so I believe he must be feeling stronger."

"That is excellent news," I said. "Now, I am finally going to go upstairs and get some rest. I might very well collapse otherwise – "

My words were cut off when a knock at the door drew the attention of us both.

I turned to look, as Mr. Tulson appeared from down near the dining room.

"I wonder who that could be," Mrs. Bell said, coming to stand beside me at the bottom of the stairs.

Mr. Tulson pulled the door open. "Good afternoon," he said. "How may I help you?"

"Pardon me..." came a woman's voice. "But is this the correct address for the private inquirer, V. M. Ward?"

Mrs. Bell and I looked at one another with surprise.

"Indeed it is," Mr. Tulson said. "However, the lady is quite busy today – "

"It's all right, Mr. Tulson," I said, already moving away down the hall. "I can speak with our guest briefly. Show her into the drawing room."

I was no sooner seated on the settee in the drawing room when Mr. Tulson appeared. "Mrs. Emsworth here to see you, madam."

"Thank you, Mr. Tulson," I said, sitting a little straighter. I could think of only one reason for a stranger to come to the house, searching for anyone by the name of Ward.

My heart beat rapidly as he stepped out, allowing a woman standing behind him to pass.

She was older than I expected, with hair like spun silver that was pinned up with a pretty amethyst pin. She wore an elegant dress of emerald green, and from the way she walked into the room, I knew right away that she was a lady of some standing. It was even possible that she may have known my parents once upon a time.

"Thank you for seeing me," the woman said. "I trust you are the V. M. Ward I have read about in the paper, and whose name I have seen advertised in shop windows?"

"That is me, yes," I said. "You may call me Miss Ward."

"Very well, Miss Ward," said Mrs. Emsworth. "I

have a request to make of a private inquirer, but I should like to say up front that this is a matter I would prefer to keep discreet. I thought by coming to someone who was lesser known, I could accomplish this."

A bit rude, that, but I suppose I can understand... "Every case of mine is kept discreet," I said. "You shall have no trouble with me. Now, why don't you tell me what it is that you need my help with?"

"Well, to be frank, Miss Ward, I am rather troubled," Mrs. Emsworth said. "You see, something very important to me has gone missing."

"Gone missing?" I asked. "What sort of something do you mean?"

"A necklace," Mrs. Emsworth said. "I would like you to find it for me. And quickly."

She began to tell me the details of the case, and I hid a small smile as I listened.

I may have finished my investigation into the killings in Hyde Park, but my career as a private inquirer, it seemed, was only just beginning. Who knew what other secrets and adventures lay ahead?

~

Continue the mysterious adventures of Victoria Sedgewick with "Death Among Fitful Shadows: The Victoria Sedgewick Mysteries, Book 3."

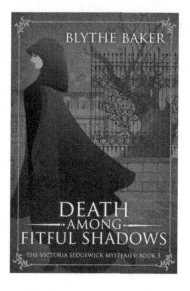

ABOUT THE AUTHOR

Blythe Baker is the lead writer behind several popular historical and paranormal mystery series. When Blythe isn't buried under clues, suspects, and motives, she's acting as chauffeur to her children and head groomer to her household of beloved pets. She enjoys walking her dogs, lounging in her backyard hammock, and fiddling with graphic design. She also likes binge-watching mystery shows on TV. To learn more about Blythe, visit her website and sign up for her newsletter at www.blythebaker.com

Made in the USA
Las Vegas, NV
06 January 2023

65122619R00104